THE DARK HORSE

Books by Will James

*

THE DARK HORSE

FLINT SPEARS

SCORPION

HOME RANCH

THE THREE MUSTANGEERS

ALL IN THE DAY'S RIDING

BIG-ENOUGH

SUN UP

LONE COWBOY

SAND

COW COUNTRY

SMOKY, THE COWHORSE

THE DRIFTING COWBOY

COWBOYS, NORTH AND SOUTH

The Uncle Bill Series

UNCLE BILL: A TALE OF TWO KIDS
AND A COWBOY

IN THE SADDLE WITH UNCLE BILL

*

YOUNG COWBOY

COWBOY IN THE MAKING

*

CHARLES SCRIBNER'S SONS

COLONEL and CHARRO

The Dark Horse

By

WILL JAMES

A MUSTANGER'S RIG

WILL JAMES

CHARLES SCRIBNER'S SONS · NEW YORK

CHARLES SCRIBNER'S SONS · LTD · LONDON

1939

Copyright, 1939, by

WILL JAMES

Printed in the United States of America

A

TO

BILL AND PEGGIE

THOROUGHBREDS

PREFACE

TO a breeder of thoroughbred horses a horse without registered pedigree is only a scrub, no matter what the looks, built or heart of him might be. The blood in cold black ink is what counts.

In this story is a horse with a pedigree a mile long and dating back to B. C. All thoroughbred and with all the qualities that goes with the meaning of that word.

With such a horse is another of no pedigree of any kind to show his worth, nothing excepting a tough hide, good heart, plenty of gumption and brains. This one is a *thoroughbred* wild horse.

These two, thoroughbreds in their own ways, are sort of throwed together by fate when still only colts, escape the human to roam and grow together in a wild, very rough and big country.

Their experiences, thru their different ways, knowledge and breeding, is such as would be with a first pilgrim and an Indian roaming the forests and plains together, and come time when neither color nor breeding mattered.

With all such experiences the best in both breeds come to the top, and in their different ways, both show what thoroughbreds they really are.

CONTENTS

ILLUSTRATIONS

THE DARK HORSE

CHAPTER ONE

THE DARK HORSE

AS it's said about a person being born with a silver spoon in the mouth and amongst all the luxuries of life, so was Colonel, a little thoroughbred colt.

There was of course no silver spoon in his mouth when he raised his head and made a little sound that was his first nicker, but the luxuries and care that surrounded him on his arrival amounted to the same as that of a prince in a kingdom of the horse world.

Half a dozen attendants was on hand to greet him to earth. The watchful mother was taken care of as well, and soon enough, as the colt showed signs of getting to his feet, he was helped up, steadied alongside of her and he took on his first nursing, seeming to bring him strength and steadiness like by magic.

He was up and a coming much quicker than his half brothers had, he was more bright eyed and alert, and for that reason he was paid more attention to than the others. Another thing was his odd and different color from his half brothers, never once before from the strong blood of his sire.

Colonel, as the colt was later named, had got his first glimpse of light in one of the well kept long string

1

green pasture that day. Ten and twelve more mares, with foals of about the same age as Colonel, all out of the same stable, was turned into the same pasture with him.

Now, with these newcomers was plenty more to make Colonel blink and wonder. He'd never seen another of his kind but his mother, neither had the other colts, and all stayed close to their mother's side and sort of stared in confusion.

But that wasn't to be for long. The mares, being green grass hungry as horses are especially during spring time, went after the tender green blades as tho their aim was to founder themselves. As they grazed and the colts sort of got their bearings and a little used to the brightness of the open they begin to get braver and make a few steps away from their mothers to ease their curiosity as to the other little colts, and get acquainted.

Colonel was about the first to step away from his mammy and come towards the colt closest to him, but he stopped halfways as that colt's mother raised her head and laid her ears back. It was only instinct that warned him of the danger of coming any closer, for he'd never seen his mother give him such a wicked look. He just stood, wondering, the mare went back to grazing and then her little colt came half ways to meet him. That seemed to be all right by the mother, and the two touched nostrils.

From then on the acquaintance was easy carried on, and now, with the company of each other they felt braver, got to playing, running around each other and their mothers, and that started things.

In a short while the other colts that'd been watching the two left their mammies, and one by one joined in. There was bowed necks as they touched nostrils, front hoofs pawed the air like for handshakes and the play was on.

And being these colts was all of the thoroughbred racing blood the play was far from slow, and even tho young as they was their thoroughbred mothers of one time track fame would of had a hard time catching up with 'em for a distance if they had a mind to. But they had no mind to, just raised their heads to watch their youngsters once in a while and went on to their grazing, knowing they'd be safe in the level and well panel-fenced pasture.

Around and around went the colts, kicking up their heels, racing out a ways, to turn, face one another, prance around some with heads and tails up and then race back, sometimes the whole bunch at once and then branching off in pairs or fours. All the actions of good race horse flesh was put on, with plenty of speed, rearing, twisting and kicking but there was no bucking, that wasn't in their blood.

Trainers and stablemen took time out to gather by the fence and watch the colts' first outing, commenting on this and that colt and their possibilities. There was great things expected of these for they was all sired by one great stallion of that stable and which had won many big stakes in handicaps and Derbys, so had some of the mares, and the colts being of such great strains should be winners. Most of 'em would be, but as is the case not all of 'em would make the grade and maybe only a few of them would win a big race, maybe none or only one out of all would be a recognized big money champion.

As the colts played and raced back and forth the men by the panel fence would remark about this and that one, and favorites was soon picked out. The colts being all straight bays and sorrels, about the same slim built and size with hardly no white markings but a small star in the forehead was hard to keep track of after being picked out, all but one. That one was dark brown in color, near black, and instead of only a star in his forehead like his half brothers had, there was a long narrow blaze that run plum to the tip of his nose. That colt was Colonel.

It was easy to pick him out from the others on account of his odd color that way but none of the men at the fence chose him as a favorite because, even tho it was only in play amongst the other colts, he never got near the lead in a straight run and sometimes trailed in last.

But not much attention was paid to that, not with colts so young and only playing. After a year or so and with some months of training it would be easier to tell as to what could be expected, and for the time the men was passing no judgment but only watching 'em more for the fun of it than any guessing as to how any of 'em would turn out.

As Colonel played and dozed during the warm summer months that followed he had no worries as to how
he might turn out, but he did have some faint idea of
what might be expected of him later on as he watched
string after string of two year olds being put to their
paces by the trainers, and being the track was right
along the pasture, him and the other colts would sometimes race along with 'em until they come to the corner,
where they would turn and race back by themselves.

He got some more ideas of what to expect as he
watched the paddocks where yearlings was being made
to run in a circle for early training, also the full grown
stallions for their daily exercise.

Then one day, along late summer, a little halter was
slipped on his head and now begin his and the other colts
to go around in circles in the paddock. Then's when he
felt the first sting of a whip. That surprised him more
than it stung, and after the first few times he trotted or
loped out of the reach of it. There was also the breaking
to lead and like all of his breed he answered to that in
short time.

A half hour or so of that every day made him feel some
different. He might cover ten miles or so during a day
of his playing but that short spell in the paddock struck
him as mighty serious business and where no foolishness
was allowed. Like with most any kid having to go to
school he was always glad to get out of the paddock and
back to the pasture to his waiting mother, nurse and
then go to grazing. He'd been eating grass for quite a
few months by then.

Days and weeks went on that way with no more accidents happening to him than a slip and a fall once in a while when at play, and that didn't count.

Then one day the big boss and owner of the stables and well known at every race track the world over as a breeder of the fine race horses, a shrewd track man, and no less a person than Morgan Mansfield himself, came to the paddock where the little colts was having their short workouts. Mansfield had just got back from a long stay in foreign lands with his family, which he'd left there, and he was so anxious to get back to his ponies that he didn't bother changing from his traveling clothes but just jumped in a car and had the chauffeur drive him around.

His eyes brightened with pleasure as he went in the paddock and looked at one after another of the slick and promising looking little colts of the spring before, every inch of 'em a thoroughbred and living pictures in flesh of their sire, the great Montezuma, a horse who'd brought him fame along with some hundred thousands on the track, sale of his colts and stud fees.

Over half the colts had been brought in and looked over with great pride and satisfaction, then another little feller acting sort of quiet was brought in, and at the sight of him, Mansfield had to look twice in surprise, and he finally asked of the trainer:

"What's that. How did *it* get in——?"

The trainer had to grin some. "Well, sir," he says, "I couldn't say but he was also sired by Montezuma and his dam is one of your best, Lady Blue. It's in the book."

"Well, well," says Mansfield, puzzled, "must be a throwback. That colt hasn't the color, action, nor resemblance of any of the others, and certainly not of Montezuma."

That was true enough. The little dark brown colt with

"What's that. How did *it* get in——?"

the blaze face was a little heavier in shoulder and forearms and thighs but mighty trim and well set up.

"But he looks like he has the makings of a good mile horse," says the trainer, "also powerful in muddy tracks."

"Maybe so," says Mansfield, frowning, "but I don't want this colt to be seen amongst the others or have it be known that he's one of Montezuma's. Put him and Lady

Blue in pasture number ten, with the other mixed colts there. I'll see to him."

So that's how come that Colonel and his mammy soon found themselves in a lower and marshy pasture, where the fences wasn't so good and the long stable was only whitewashed, all amongst big trees and pretty well hid. It was a kind of third grade pasture but Colonel only enjoyed the change, and being outcast from his half brothers didn't have no effect on him. He soon made friends with some other colts of his own age there, and even tho they was no kin of his he had as much play and fun as before, only there was more flies from the marshes, but to make up for that there was less regular nor no stiff paddock work.

The chill of fall begin to come, nights got plenty cool, and Colonel's half brothers was now being kept in their luxurious box stalls during such nights, fed special and groomed. But not with Colonel nor the ones he was pasturing with. Them was left to stay out in the pasture, and even tho there was still plenty of grass there was no special feed nor warm stalls when chilly nights come and cold winds blowed, but there was good shelter in the thick brush and they could make out without much suffering, until winter really set in, when they would then be stabled and well fed, but the only heat would be from their own bodies.

But before the real cold winds and snow begin to come and winter did set in, Colonel was weaned from his mother and one day loaded in a horse trailer, whizzed north some few hundred miles to a big stock yards where he was led to a stall and kept like in solitary confinement.

It all happened mighty sudden, and little Colonel sure couldn't make out what this was all about. The fast and long scary ride in the trailer, then being led thru stock-yard lanes into a big shed-like stable and tied up to the manger of a narrow, dark and musty stall had him pretty well spooked as to what would be next. Every time he'd hear footsteps come near or by his dark stall he'd nicker soft for some kind of explaining he might under-stand, or at least be untied and left loose in one of the big corrals he'd passed and adjoining the many horses he'd seen in them. He'd never been tied up before, never been away from the company of other horses, and worse yet was how he missed his mother, for he hadn't been weaned away from her but only a few days when he was taken north, away from her and his playmates to be dumped in the dark hole where he was, all by his lone-some.

The man who'd brought him north came to see him on the next day, there was another man with him. Colonel was untied, led out blinking into the sunlight and made to trot and lope around a big square corral. This suited him fine and he would of liked to kept running some more to limber up after the long night's stay in the stall, but he was stopped while the two men confabbed for a spell. The stranger, a short, fat and dark man, wearing thick glasses, made a lot of motions as he talked, then finally shook his head, put his hands in his overcoat pockets and walked away.

Another stranger was brought along later that day

and then another after that. Each time, Colonel was led out of his dark stall and made to trot and lope some more in the big corral, and by the time he was thru for that day he felt a little tired, more hungry and less worried. He didn't mind the dark and damp stall so much that night.

The next day brought him the same chance to exercise and limber up, and at one time there was three strangers came, when he had to do more running around than usual. He at first wondered what this was all about but all he got out of it was that he again felt a little tired when night come, more hungry than before, and ever since he was taken away from his home pastures, and on that third night of his confinement was his first time to lay down and sleep while tied to a manger.

Two more strangers was brought along at different times the next day, and with the second ones, Colonel's little heart missed a beat and then pumped fast as that one came near and touched him. There was no cold, far off ways about him as with the strangers that'd come before, and then, more to Colonel's surprise and pleasure there was a good strong horse smell on that stranger's rough jacket, even on his broad brim hat. The other strangers that'd come before had a smell that only made him want to wrinkle up his nose and sneeze.

Colonel was left to stand as the two men begin to talk and then's when he figured was a good time to take a roll, he hadn't had a chance to have one since leaving the home pastures to the south. He got down to his knees to proceed to do that, when the man who'd handled him north started to make a motion to stop him, but the stranger stopped that motion, saying:

"Aw, let the little feller roll."

"But I just groomed him good this morning."

"Well, you can groom him again," grinned the stranger.

So, with no interruption, Colonel went to rolling to his heart's content, the stranger squatted by the side of the corral and rolling a cigarette watched him, then he spoke up sudden while the colt was enjoying himself.

"I'll give you a hundred dollars for him every time he rolls clear over."

The stranger held out his hand for the other to shake and like to bind the deal. The colt had already rolled over twice and while the other man hesitated to take the offer he rolled over once more. That decided him, and now hoping he would roll over once or twice more he took the stranger's hand, saying "That's a deal."

Horses seldom roll over more than twice, but with this active colt having been tied up and not being used to that it might be, but not at all likely, that he'd go five times.

After the third time, Colonel stood up, shook himself. But all wasn't over, and the two men kind of held their breath in suspense as the colt went to his knees and down, like to roll over some more. It was now the stranger's turn to wish he wouldn't and the other's that he would. The stranger won, for the colt didn't roll over no more, just sort of halfways and only scratched himself in the corral dirt.

Colonel had rolled over just enough times to put over

the deal and no more. But now that deal didn't seem satisfactory to the track man, and being there was no papers made to that agreement mere words didn't count, not when that gentleman figured on getting one or two hundred dollars more, and he spoke up to that effect.

"I'm sorry, Bo——" he begins with a queer grin, then he was interrupted.

"I'm no Bo," says the stranger, sensing what was coming. "My name is Brad, Bradley Braddock and you can make me a bill of sale for that colt to that name."

"Well, B-Brad," says the other man, not much disturbed, "mine is Jerry, and what I was going to say is that I'm sorry but I can't let you have this colt, not for three hundred."

The man Brad was sort of dumfounded at that, and the other noticing the expression of his face, hurried on to explain that the colt wasn't his, that he was only selling him for somebody else whose name wasn't to be let out on account of him being so well known as ace high in race horse breeding, that this colt was sired from his best horse, had the papers to prove it, and none had brought less than five thousand dollars at six months of age when taken away from the dam.

This colt being of odd color, the man Jerry went on, and being of different built than the others by the famous sire is the reason why he was taken out of the country and to be rid of on account he might reflect on the sire's blood which would hurt with the sale of his other colts.

But it was expected that, even without showing the papers proving the colt's pedigree, his appearance alone showed his fine breeding and be enough proof so he would sell for at least a thousand. Much more than that could of been got by just showing the papers but that wasn't to be done.

The stranger, Brad seemed to be some little impressed by the story. He was quiet for a spell when the other got thru talking, then he pointed to some corrals filled with horses some distance in the big yards.

"See them horses?" he says. "Well, they're the ones you seen buck at the rodeo grounds, where you met me. They're going to be loaded tonight and shipped." He then pointed at the colt. "This little feller will be going along with 'em and so far west before he's unloaded that he'll just as well be in China for all you and your boss will ever see or hear of him."

"Now, getting back to our deal, you and me shook hands on it and I'm not going to let you back out. I took a chance and was willing to put out a hundred more than I intended to on the colt without knowing what he is. You agreed to take a chance too, figuring the colt would roll to four or five times—You being wise to gambling on the ponies ought to be used to taking chances, and this is one time when you lost.

"But not altogether. You let me see the slip where you have a right to sell this colt, write me out a bill of sale for him and I'll split the difference with you between the three hundred I was to pay you and the five hundred you was doing high gambling to get."

The track man squirmed a bit at that but he also seen where he couldn't very well squirm out. So, making the

And that night, Colonel wasn't tied up to no manger in no dark and damp stall

best of it he handed out the paper of release for sale of the colt. It was typed on plain paper but the name of the stables where the colt was from and the signature of the overseer of them was at the bottom, and at that, the stranger's face lit up in surprise.

"Well, I'll be hornswoggled," he says. "Old U-Bet Mansfield's stables——"

"How do you know?" asks the other, also very surprised, and sort of upset.

"How do I know? Well I got hurt at a rodeo in this same town a couple of years ago. I'd got to know him before once when he came west and was to a rodeo there and other times, and when I got layed up here there was no chance of talking him out of me coming to his place and recuperate, and now I'll tell you what you don't want to tell me, it's that this colt's sire is none other than Montezuma. Am I right?

"But," he went on, "you and Mansfield don't have to worry about his identity being spread, I think a whole lot of Mansfield and noboy will ever know, not from me, who I got this colt from and who his sire is. I'm just going to make a good rope horse out of him and I think he'll do fine for fast straight away contest work. Now let me see his registration papers, just for my own satisfaction."

They was now handed to him without hesitation, and being very satisfactory the two then walked to the yard office, the bill of sale was written in the back of the paper releasing the colt, witnessed and signed—and that night, Colonel wasn't tied up to no manger in no dark and damp stall.

CHAPTER TWO

GO WEST, YOUNG MAN

A MIXED freight was puffing its way acrost the long stretches of the Great Plains and against a cold west wind. Amongst the mixed freight cars was six stock cars loaded with strange stock, the kind no stockman nor farmer could or had any use for, for outside of one carload of top saddle horses which no money nor love could buy, the rest was worse than useless for work of any kind besides being dangerous to handle. They was outlaw bucking horses used in rodeos, and there they was plenty good.

In other cars was mean bulls of all breeds and for the same purpose, then wiry longhorn steers, some also used for bucking, roping and bull-dogging.

It was a mixed up bunch of wise, wild and tough ones and the least kind where a thin-skin, blue-blood thoroughbred colt would be expected to be found amongst. But sure enough, at one end of a long stock car of buckers, and partitioned off from them by stout timbers so he wouldn't be got down and tromped on, was such a little colt. It was Colonel, headed west in that carload of "toughs," the cream of the racing blood amongst the cream of the worst of the West. The first night had been a scary one for Colonel as he was loaded, stuck away

into his partition and then the big snaky outlaws was
made to come up the loading chute and into the same
car with him, snorting and fighting as they came into
the door. It was some more scary as the car was jerked
in switching, big black steam belching and fiery mon-
sters of engines going back and forth close past him,
and it was a good thing his partition was high and the
timbers close together or he'd gone over or thru it.
As it was he just had to stand where he was, legs wide
apart, wild eyed and trembling with fear at all the noise
of the big switch yards, shrill whistles and blinding
lights. His only bit of assurance was the close company
of the big horses and he'd every once in a while stick
his little nose thru the timbers and touch the one next
to him with his nostrils.

It eased him some that the big outlaws didn't seem
nervous nor fret none in any way. And they shouldn't,
for being loaded in cars shipped and unloaded in strange
places to do their worst at different rodeos was nothing
new to the most of 'em. That was done many times a
year during the contesting season, which east of the
Rockies starts about July and ends along about October,
and west of the Rockies plum down to Texas where
there's rodeos off and on all winter.

This bunch of rodeo stock wasn't to go west of the
Rockies but would be unloaded and taken to their home
range on the eastern slope of 'em for the winter, where
they'd be well taken care of and be in fine shape for the
following year's round of rodeos.

After at last pulling out of the big noisy railroad

yards and the train begin to go on its way smooth,
Colonel, even tho mighty puzzled at going over ground
without moving a hoof, felt much less scared only when
getting into some more big railroad yards again, or
when some fast train would swish by sudden while on
the way. It was a good thing he had a stout heart at
such times.

On the third day and when the Great Plains was
reached was another time when his pulse beat some
faster, but not from scare now, it was from the sight of
big wide stretches of level land without a tree nor even
a bush nowheres in sight, just grass. In all his life of
six months or so he'd never seen such big, level and open
country. The train was doing good speed and he'd liked
to got out and raced with it, or better yet, with some of
the playmates he'd been taken away from back in the
home pastures.

He didn't think he'd care to race or play with the big
mean looking horses that was in the same car with him.
They struck him as very strange in looks and action
from any horse he'd ever seen. Like the big gray next
to him for instance, he'd seen him and the others run
away from the sight of man when unloaded to be fed
and watered in the big feed yards along the way, making queer rolling and whistling noises at 'em. The horses
he knew would follow man instead of running away,
and liked to be petted. But not these.

This big gray had already killed two men and was
always watching his chance to get another, like many
more in the same car. He was a natural born outlaw with

All the western horse wants is his freedom

roman nose, small sunken eyes, heavy jaws and tight under lip. As to his built it was as much that of a fighter as any boxer that ever entered a ring. The others varied some in size and built but all had more or less the same earmarks of the outlaw. Not "made" outlaws by any cruelty or mistreatment, or goaded to meanness as some people *seem to want* to think, but born with a natural kink leaning that way, just as some humans are.

The western horse being raised free and wild, and

with many generations of wild blood in his veins is very independent of man. He's not like his eastern brother who looks to man for his food and shelter, like the ancestors of little Colonel for instance. All the western horse wants is his freedom. He'll fight for that, and some fight so well that they finally wind up in rodeo arenas to do their stuff there. Many of them are well bred horses nowdays, but being born free, raised in the open, and with still a little strain of the wild blood in their veins is plenty to do the trick, many of 'em want to stay that way.

There's scarce cases where some horses that are willing to be good are goaded to buck and be mean. It's a good thing such cases *are* scarce. Such lowdown cowardly doings is very much against true cowboy principle and never practiced by one. For there's plenty of natural mean horses without making a good one so.

As the train headed on acrost the Plains and a cold wind, with a clean sweep, blowed thru the slats of the stock car, little Colonel sort of lost his thrill at the sight of so big and level a country. All he seen in it now was how he'd liked to run and play on it and only warm up, for he was getting mighty cold. His thin hide and fine boned body wasn't for such blasts which seemed to go right thru him, and as the day wore on and stinging snow begin to drift in he got so cold and to shivering that he'd been glad to take the chance of squeezing between the big outlaws for warmth.

The coming night was to be still colder, and Colonel might of froze stiff, but that evening the train came to a stop at some more big stock yards, and more switch engines to scare him. With all of that he was now shivering fit for his bones to rattle apart, when he heard a familiar voice which he nickered at with a mighty plain sound of distress.

Brad had to laugh a little at the loud and plain call for help, because that's just what he'd come for, to help him, and what made him laugh was the such a loud call from such a little feller, also how he showed he recognized him. It was the first time he'd nickered at his coming.

The outlaw broncs only snorted as Brad had walked along the car, stopped to look thru the slats at the little wild-eyed, shivering colt and went to talking to him.

"Well, little feller," he says, noticing his shivering. "It don't go so good being away from steam heated stables this time a year, does it? Better start growing a fur coat, but hang on a spell and I'll soon fix you up with the next best."

This was another feed yard, and in a short time the horses and cattle was unloaded in separate pens where plenty of hay and water was ready for them. Soon as the broncs was out of the car where the colt was, Brad came in with a couple of heavy padded horse blankets, each one big enough for two the size of Colonel, but they sure would do to cover him up well and keep him warm in most any weather, if he could stand up under the weight of 'em. He of course could, and he'd still be only the warmer if he layed down.

Fastening a rope on the halter, Brad led the shivering colt out of the stall and at once put one of the blankets on him then shoved up a bucket of warm water which he'd heated on the caboose stove, and while the colt was drinking he begin to fix the blankets on him so they'd be sure to stay. With cinches, latigoes and tie ropes from his saddle he went to work on fastening the blankets, and he had to laugh some again in trying to find the colt underneath all the covering. When he got thru all there could be seen of him was his ankles and his head, and his ankles would also be covered when back in his stall, for Brad brought in a couple of fork-fuls of waste hay for bedding, also good hay for him to feed on. Another bucketful of warm water which the colt couldn't finish and by then he'd well stopped shivering.

Satisfied that the colt would now be sure enough all right he took him back to his stall and to the fresh hay he'd put for him there, refastened the timbers good and solid and then left him to go take care of his own self and stomach at the depot restaurant acrost the tracks, where two other cowboys who was along with him to take care of the stock, help load and unload 'em, was now enjoying a smoke after eating their fill. They couldn't wait for him while he took care of his "urchin," they said.

The stock having their fill of hay and water, many of 'em now laying down, was again stirred, loaded and the train was once more on its way. One more feeding stop and the stock, after another day and night on the

train, would be unloaded again. This time to be trailed
to their home range.

Even tho it was mighty cold, Colonel sure didn't feel
none of it that night, not after the way Brad had
bundled him so. Well filled up and no stops or switching
to disturb him much he dozed on his feet, and then,
maybe on account of the weight of the blankets, he layed
down to sound sleep a couple of times and, as is said,
was "snug as a bug in a rug."

The rest of the trip was no more hardship to him,
but there was still some more to come which he had to
buck thru. When after another day and night, the train
came to a last stop for the stock, and all was unloaded
at their home country's yards at the break of day, there
was a heavy gray sky and near a foot of snow to greet
'em. Looked like there was more to come soon.

And sure enough, the stock had no more than got
their fill of hay and water and little rest when it did
start to snow again. Colonel, still blanketed and fed
separate from the others, didn't seem to mind, not until
Brad came along and stripped his pack some for travel,
remarking that he'd need his cinchas to put back on his
saddle and that now one blanket would do him, for he'd
be keeping plenty warm bucking thru the deep snow
on the rest of the way to the ranch. So, he left only one
blanket on him, folded it to cover him well from the
withers back of his hips and wouldn't be hindered in
his travelling, squaw-hitched it on to stay, and as the
buckers and saddle horses was turned out of the yards
and headed on the last stretch of the trip, Colonel was

led on a ways and then turned loose with 'em, with a
grinning warning from Brad not to let any of the rough
broncs chew his tail off and run him down in a snow
bank.

The cattle was brought along separate by a couple
of other cowboys sent from the ranch, and even tho the
weather was plenty cold, all the stock lined out in fine
shape. They was all go for travel on the hoof and limber
up after so many long days and nights of standing in
the cars, and all knew of the good sheltered winter range
they was headed for, all excepting Colonel.

The colt was some leary when he was turned loose to
join in with the big and wicked looking horses, and when
he appeared amongst 'em and many turned and circled
around him he figured sure his end had come. He sort
of cringed, squatted and ducked as some fought their
way thru the circle to get a close look at him, and as
colts do when timid in meeting strange horses, Colonel's
mouth opened wide, and worked much as a forced smile
and like wanting to be friendly, very much so.

But Colonel didn't need to have any fear, for the big
fellers hadn't been near any little colts since away the
spring before. Their company was always more or less
fought for, sometimes even with the colts' mothers, and
they was only curious and pleased at the sight of the
new, blanketed little feller.

The blanket around Colonel's middle at this time not
only protected him from the weather but also kept the
big horses from coming too close, for that blanket was
something they didn't like the looks of, no more than

they did a saddle or anything belonging to humans. So, keeping their distance they only touched nostrils with him.

But that was still too close to suit Colonel, and he'd tried to make a break out of reach but there was no going thru the circle that surrounded him, and he got sort of panicky.

Brad stopped his horse at a distance and watched, knowing that no harm would come to the colt and that once their curiosity was satisfied and acquaintance made they would jog on without paying much more attention to him. But that circle was to be broke up, quick and before Brad had decided to. . . . The big gray killer coming to see what the "meeting" was all about, and noticing the colt, soon scattered himself an opening to him. Him and the colt having already been sort of acquainted thru the heavy timbers of the partition in the stock car sort of made it easy for the both getting together again, and the big outlaw being used to see the blanket on the colt didn't spook at it, then the colt recognizing his traveling pardner felt much relieved to have him near, also to see the opening in the circle. When the big gray took the lead on, Colonel was glad to follow.

He followed on close by his side at first, for he felt safe near him, sensed that the big gray was the boss over the other horses and would protect him from them, still not knowing he didn't need to have any fear of the others, and that any of them would of also liked to've had his company. He learned that later.

Getting closer and traveling along the foothills the

snow got deeper, up to Colonel's knees in some places, and as he begin to tire some he then got behind the big gray who proved to be not only a mighty good trail breaker but also a break to the wind and the stinging snow.

Colonel had never been "herd-broke," meaning that he'd never been driven loose to any distance with a bunch of horses before. At his home pastures he'd most always been haltered and led, and if it'd been tried to drive him with a bunch he'd went where he pleased and took a good run by himself. But now it seemed very much that he should stick to the trail and the bunch he was with, for he was in a very strange, big, and desolate looking country, the snow was deep and drifting and he less than cared to break away from the trail of the big gray. He was now, and without his knowing, being herd-broke, and would stay with a driven bunch any time from then on, even when the grass would come green, the sun by shining warm and he would feel like running.

He got more education in herd-breaking as the day wore on with steady traveling up and down hills, winding thru pine, skirting tall cliffs and on and on. He was getting tired and begin to lag behind the gray, and only the sight and fear of another horse close to him would make him catch up. But soon he seen that they neither would harm him, and so he lagged on, horse after horse passed him and he finally got so far behind as to the shoulder of Brad's horse.

Brad looked down at him and grinned a little, and like in encouragement, he says:

"Kind of tough going, ain't it, little feller?"

He reached over and patted him on the snow covered rump. "But keep a going, we've only got a few miles to go and then we'll stop for the night."

The sound of Brad's voice and the feel of a human hand didn't do as was expected, for instead of jumping ahead as western-bred colts would do, Colonel stopped still in his tracks, side-glanced up at Brad and nickered low. For right then, and as was his breeding, he'd rather have the company of humans than that of horses.

Knowing horses as Brad did, horses of all kinds, he'd no more than spoke when he realized he shouldn't, then the colt would of went on, maybe slow but he'd went on. Now with hearing the voice and feeling the hand of a human the blood of the colt's long line of fine bred ancestors showed up in him mighty plain and sudden. It all at once meant security, warmth, food and rest, and he'd stopped as if that attention would come to him right there and then.

The question now was to getting him to moving on. There was no slapping him with the quirt, for, for one thing, Brad couldn't think of doing that, and another was that the colt was still too young to understand what that would of meant. He'd soon got to know what the sting of a whip lash meant while going thru the short workouts in the paddocks of his home land. That was along with his breeding, and true to form he took to his early training natural.

But here it was different, there was no paddock nor race track nor strings of long stables. To him, a whole lot of queer things had happened since he'd been taken away from his mother only a couple of weeks before, it'd been all scary and confusing. He was still confused, besides being cold, hungry and mighty tired, and it was no wonder he was so ready to answer to Brad's touch and voice, that'd sort of cleared everything in his mind and jerked him away from the nightmare he'd been plugging along on thru.

Now seeing that the harm had already been done, Brad spoke to him more. "Sorry, little feller," he says. "I wish I could pick you up and carry you along but you're too much horse, and somehow you got to make it on your own legs. Sure can't stay here."

That talk had no effect on the colt only to make him perk his ears up some, but the cold wind and stinging snow soon made him bow his head down against it some more.

There he stood, and for a minute, Brad didn't know just what to do. He sure wasn't any too warm himself. Finally and talking to him some more he started his horse, hoping the colt would follow by the sound of his voice. But outside of just raising his head and looking around like lost as Brad rode on he made no move to follow, and that cowboy sort of lost hope. He then rode on a little farther and called to him, and that done the trick, the colt nickered and after a while caught up with him.

Brad talked as he rode on and even sang a little. He also tried to whistle for a change but the cold had stiffened his mouth so that was impossible.

The colt came on to his talk but mighty slow, and finally, Brad being left away behind with him, rode up to the two other riders and told 'em to go on with the horses, that he'd stay with the colt and try to get him into camp by dark.

"All right," says one of the boys, grinning thru snow-bound whiskers. "How do you like your eggs for breakfast, straight up or turned over easy?"

"Yep, and should we warm up some milk for the urchin?" says the other.

With only a grin for answer, Brad rode back to where he'd left the colt, and to his surprise the colt had followed his trail quite a ways and acted like he wanted to travel. But Brad wasn't to be fooled by that. He knew that the colt was near all in, had just got kind of spooked at finding himself alone and came on the best he could. It had been then that a spark of a long unused instinct had come back to him, the instinct of trailing.

Keeping at a short distance ahead, Brad talked to him. At that the colt perked up, nickered and came on some more. He kept on a coming, slow and staggering but a coming, until finally, seeing that he couldn't make it much farther, and coming to a sheltered spot amongst tall cottonwoods and a bare spot against bordering rims, Brad stopped and got off his horse, the colt edged close, smelled of the bare earth and right away went down to his knees then flat on his side.

Brad looked down at him and then to his horse. "Well, Roper," he says, "it looks like we'll have to make camp here for a spell. Good thing we're at least on a bare

spot and in good shelter. Going to dig up a little heat
now."

With all the dead, dry timber and branches close by
it was no time when a fire was built and the crackling
of it went to echoing along the sheltering rim and trees
on the deep wash. The colt blinked at the fire a bit, felt
its warmth, then his eyes closed and he went to a sound
sleep. Roper followed suit by cocking one leg and
snoozed standing up, then taking one look at the two
and not to be outdone, Brad drug a few more heavy
limbs across the fire, they'd do for a long time, curled
up to within arms' reach of the colt and also was soon
asleep.

It was near dark when he woke up, the fire had burned
low, and throwing some light branches on it soon had
it going again. He rolled a smoke while noticing the
colt's eyes again blinking at the light and fresh blaze
of the stirred fire. Soon he stretched at the warmth and
at that there was hope he'd be able to make it the rest
of the way into camp. Roper had hardly moved a hoof
but now was wide awake and looking like as much as to
say. "When do we eat?"

Warmed up some more and seeming more rested, the
colt raised his head and begin looking around.

"That's the spirit," says Brad to him. "Now
stand up on them long legs of yours, and let's move
on."

The colt didn't stand up at just that, he only yawned
wide and like he could sleep some more, but Brad had
other ideas. He walked to him, felt of the thick blanket

Brad drug a few more heavy limbs across the fire, they'd do for a long time, curled up to within arms' reach of the colt and also was soon asleep

which was now dry and warm and then slapped him on
the rump, saying. "Get up, you lazy bum."

The first slap didn't do no good, neither did the order.
It took a couple more slaps and stiffer orders, and then
the colt, seeing the cowboy meant it, finally got to his
feet, bowed his neck, stretched some more, and by that,
Brad took hope he'd easy enough make it the rest of
the way in, he thought.

But the weather and now still deeper snow had to be
accounted for, and Brad, after getting out of the shelter
and warmth of the fire, seen that a near blizzard was
sweeping acrost country. It had also got even colder.
The tracks of the other horses was drifted over, and
now, with the blinding snow which would have to be
faced, Brad couldn't expect the colt to follow by just
talking to him, for the talk couldn't of been heard in
the howling wind.

So, the next best, which would be the only sure way
not to lose him in the storm would be to lead him. Fastening a lead rope to his halter, straightening up the
blanket to stay and for all protection possible, Brad
moved him around some to sort of limber him up and
get him ready to face the "outside." Then getting on
his horse the outfit started out.

As Brad figured, it was only now about an hour's
ride* to camp, but in this weather and with the colt's
slow travelling against the storm and deep snow it would
be at least two hours before it could be reached. But

*An hour's ride is gaged pretty well by what's called dog trot and
fast walk, which is about five miles.

there the colt sort of surprised him, for he led up and bucked the storm in good shape. The rest and warming up had sure done its work, and if there'd been some nourishment in his tummy he'd done still better.

As Brad rode along, cold, head bent against the storm, he thought of just that, nourishment, not so much for himself as for the colt and Roper. There was no hay for the horses nor stable or even a shed where he was headed for to spend the rest of the night, the place was just a line camp and the only building on it was a one-room, dirt-roof log cabin, with stove, grub and bunks. There was of course a round corral and a good-sized fenced in pasture where standing feed was saved for the riders' horses also for whatever stock was wanted held there on the way to or from the shipping point.

There was also good shelter in the pasture, but as Brad rode on, the blizzard getting fiercer and hardly being able to see any further than his horse's ears, he kept a wondering about the colt and how he'd make out in that storm for the rest of the night and the next day. And the colt, like steady reminding was now beginning to tug more and more on the rope. He was fast getting tired again. But there could be no more stopping, for being there was no kind of shelter until camp was reached, stopping would mean sure freezing to death.

As it was now, with the blinding storm and darkness, nothing to go by excepting the direction of the wind, which might change any time and cause the rider to go astray, it would have to be more than luck if the line camp was located, no stranger could of. For even with

Jerked on the latch string at the same time and in he went
pulling the colt inside right after him

Brad, as well as he knew the country, there was none of it for him to see so as to recognize, and he depended most altogether on Roper's judgment and instinct to find camp. That horse had made the trip many times from the ranch to the shipping point and back, and a compass would of been more than useless as compared to him there.

Brad had rode many long miles in that country, miles that when thirsty, hungry or cold seemed more like five than one. But these last few miles that night was the longest he'd ever rode, for he now had more than himself to consider. The colt was steady hanging back more and more on the rope and weaving from side to side in his tracks as tho he might fall any time. Brad worried with fear that he would, for if he did it would about be impossible to get him up and going again, and there being no shelter nor anything to make a fire in that particular bleak and open stretch it would sure mean the end of him. There would be no way of even hauling him in.

With the lead rope to the saddle horn, Roper was near dragging the colt, step by step and very slow, when at last, Brad faintly seen the line camp's fence and no sight had ever meant so much to that cowboy, none that he could of thought of right then.

On account of the storm being so thick, Roper had been the first to see, or sense, the fence and along it he went pulling the colt until, finally the gate was reached.

Once there, and coming to a stop to open the gate, Brad knew what would happen, and it did. Roper no more than stopped pulling on the rope when down went the colt, and this time it looked like to stay.

But Brad wouldn't have it that way, not when he finally had him so close to home. He went to work on him and slapped him hard from neck to rump to keep the blood circulating and to get him up, and at last, with a couple more slaps along the neck, some talking to, another pull on the lead rope the colt straightened his front legs, Brad pulled some more and he stood up again.

There was no taking any chances of letting him get down no more, and being the cabin was only a couple of hundred yards away he made for it, pulling on the rope for all he was worth, Roper dragging the bridle reins and following.

There was no stop again, not even when the cabin door was reached, for Brad made a lunge for it, jerked on the latch string at the same time and in he went pulling the colt inside right after him, then he closed the door.

"Where's them fried eggs?" he hollered at the other riders as they'd jumped up at the sudden commotion, lit a candle and rubbed their eyes at the sight of the snow covered man and colt.

CHAPTER THREE

A STRANGE PORT IN A STORM

THE morning was well along before there was good
enough light of day in the line camp so the boys
could see by. But they'd been up for quite a spell, and
by candle light had cooked and et a good breakfast of
hot biscuits and bacon, washed down with plenty of
black coffee (no eggs).

There hadn't been much steady sleep for the boys
that night. Without bedding, they'd stretched out on
the hay-filled, nailed-to-the-wall, two-story bunks and
took only their chaps off, which was used for covering
on legs and feet. The old line camp being used mostly
during summers hadn't been kept very weather tight,
the daubing and chinking was gone in some places and
the snow driven hard by cold winds sifted in between
the logs and made fair sized snowbanks on the floor and
bunks.

But it was very much better than being outside at
that. The little tin stove which heated quick and died
near as quick was kept a going most of the time by one
or the other of the boys, waking up at being chilled,
would get up and tend to it. The coffee pot was heated
each time, a cup of it, a cigarette and all was comfortable
again for a spell.

All, including the colt, which now being out of the

storm and even tho his blanket taken off of him, was very comfortable at all times. The blanket had been switched onto Roper's back soon as the saddle was pulled off, was given a double feed of the grain which was kept stored in steel drums for that purpose, and backed against the cabin for a wind break was also some comfortable.

Inside, it had taken the colt some time to rest and warm up. He'd of course layed or fell down near as soon as the door had been closed after him, and when some hours later he revived enough to raise his head to look around and his nose brushed against some hay was when he revived some more. It was hay padding the lower bunk where Brad was laying, and no telling of how long it'd been there.

So's the colt wouldn't be running into things or falling over the stove during the night, Brad had tied him to his bunk, and that went well with him, especially after he'd thawed out and got a whiff of the hay in that bunk, and even tho that whiff told him the hay was old, matted and broken fine in some places from much laying on it was hay, and he was mighty hungry.

He et all the hay to within his reach while laying down then he got up to get more, and Brad, feeling him nosing around his feet edged closer to the wall and kicked some more his way, feeling relieved that the colt was up and a coming again.

When him and the other boys got up to cook and eat breakfast the colt had about cleaned up the foot end of the bunk and also reached up to get what more

And also reached up to get what more hay was hanging over the edge
of the bunk above

hay was hanging over the edge of the bunk above.

"I've heard of folks being et out of house and home," says the rider who'd used the bunk as he climbed down from it, "but I never heard of anybody having their bedding et out from under 'em while they slept."

"That's all right now," Brad grinned. "Don't cry. I'll feed the culprit so he wont touch your bedding any more."

So, while the boys et their breakfast, the colt was also eating his, it was grain which Brad had placed on the flooring of the bunk.

Roper, still in the shelter of the cabin, was later taken care of with another good feed of grain. But it took a little time to get to him, for as Brad opened the door he was met by a wind so stiff that he had a hard time closing it again, and at a space to one side of the cabin was a drift from four to eight feet deep in places. But Roper wasn't suffering any, he was in a space between the drift and the cabin and was now well surrounded with shelter, and with the good feed of grain he'd fare along well. So well, Brad thought, that he'd turn the colt out with him after a spell, when it might get warmer and the blizzard let up some.

But as one after another of the boys went out in the storm to either dig up the wood pile and chop some wood or get some water at the open spring below the cabin they returned in a sort of hurry to hug the stove, shaking their heads as they stomped their feet and warmed their hands, remarking that the storm was even worse than it'd been the evening before and it'd be about impossible to get the horses out of the shelter they now was in and make them face it, which they would have to do all the rest of the way to the ranch.

"There'd be only one way," says one of the boys as he reached for the steaming coffee pot, "and that'd be to make 'em back all the way."

That was said so serious that the other boys was caught looking foolish for at first believing he really meant it.

But it was seen there could be no going on, not in that storm. It was one of these first heavy storms that usually come in the fall of the year or early part of winter, after which the weather most always turns and stays good for a month or so, or till winter really sets in.

There's no telling how long such storms might last, sometimes they'll blow themselves out in a day and then again they might last off and on for a couple of weeks.

If it let up by noon, the boys thought they could still make the ranch with the horses some time during the night. In the meantime they'd busy themselves at cooking up something to do for the noon and evening meal, something besides bacon and biscuits. But being nothing is kept in such camps that would freeze there wasn't much in variety to cook, only rice, beans, raisins and dried apples, all put in cans to keep from the pack rats.

While what was to be cooked was being decided on, Brad had set a bucket of water on the stove to get the chill off and gave it to the colt which he drank right down, but he couldn't quite finish another one. It was then Roper's turn and that horse had Brad pack three of them thru the storm to the spring, back to the stove and then out to him before his thirst was quenched. It was a lot of fuss maybe but to Brad and in such weather them ponies was sure worth it.

It was along near noon when Brad, going out again, this time for his share of wood cutting, thought the wind had of a sudden warmed up considerable. It was as strong as ever and still bringing snow but it had all the feelings of a coming chinook to him, only it was still coming from the same direction and there was no telling as yet.

Anyhow it wasn't so cold now, he thought, so the cold couldn't be out for a while anyway, and so long as he wouldn't have to buck the drifts in steady travelling it'd do him good and only limber him up.

So the colt was led out in the whirling snow again, brought in the shelter alongside of Roper and there that good horse was parted with his blanket. It was again squaw-hitched to cover the colt, for coming out of the warm cabin would of been sort of hard on his thin hide without that blanket. Besides, Roper being born and raised in that country had seldom been blanketed, and he'd spent many a long winter on the open range there, coming out slick and fat at spring time.

Rice and bacon mixed, hot biscuits and coffee, then another mixture of rice and raisins for dessert and plenty more coffee made up a good and warming noon meal, then the boys stretched out on the bunks to just relax some, smoke and talk, and feeling sure the storm would last and so they couldn't hit out that day there was nothing for them to do but that, just talk or sleep for a while.

The talk was started with that of the weather, when one of the boys remarked that if he had some of that steam heat which was at them hotels in the East pocketed in a way so he could use it as he rode he'd start out with the horses, blizzard or no blizzard.

"That dont make sense." Brad, acting serious, "How about the horses? I expect you'd want a steam heated corral on wheels to drive 'em in."

That didn't make sense either but it started the talk, and talking of steam heat took 'em back to the East where they'd just been for a couple of weeks, to attend a big rodeo. They'd had some fun there and came back with less than what they went with, even after the hard contesting they'd done and winnings they'd made. Brad had been the only one to come back with something to show for the trip. He'd won first money in both bronc and steer riding, and with his expenses and buying the colt he came back with about half of his winnings.

Brad's buying of the colt had been a puzzle to the two riders, and if they knew how much he'd paid for him it would of been away beyond a puzzle. It would of been a plain case of where he should be tied down, his head examined and his money taken away from him, for as they said, "mighty fine range colts of this one's age could be got for ten and twenty dollars, and not spindle-legged things that have to be babied, blanketed and brought into the house like a house plant every time a cool breeze came up."

"Anyhow I'll bet he'll come to outrun any horse in this country," Brad had answered, "and he'll make good time in contest roping."

That last had brought a snort from one of the boys and the other agreed with him when he said, "I'd be scared stiff to rope a sick rabbit from him for fear he'd be jerked down or break a leg when the rope tightened, let alone roping and stopping a big husky yearling calf."

Talking about rodeos and then the colt again in the line camp that stormy day, Brad was finally asked just how much he was paid to "take that colt way." Sure nobody what knew horses would pay real money for any such.

That of a sudden made Brad wonder if them boys knew how much he did pay for the colt. But hardly thinking so he answered that what he paid for him wasn't much as compared to what he'd win with him and let it go at that.

"You wait till you see him step out and make fast time in roping," he went on, "then you fellers will be laughing the other way."

"How long will we have to wait and who's going to take care of him while he's growing. You're gone most of the time and you know that Cal (the ranch owner) wont allow him to stay in the bunk house with us."

All three grinned, and the talk went on as to the prospects of the coming winter. Jim, one of the boys, was for staying at the ranch and just make a hand of himself. He'd been to enough contests the past summer to do him for a long spell. As for Red, the other rider, he was sort of undecided and would wait until Brad crossed the mountains, and let him know how the land layed as to contests there, how many and what the prizes would be in that warmer land along the coast on down to the Border.

There wouldn't be much doing in rodeos until after the first of the year, but up to that time there'd be considerable doing in range work, and so, Brad and Jim and Red was always welcome on the Cal Goodwin outfit, known the country around as the Hip O (circle on hip bone). That brand was for cattle only, there was many different horse brands.

The three riders had worked for the Hip O off and on for some years. They was three good cowboys, good on the range as well as on the rodeo grounds, and Cal Goodwin had all faith in their handling of his bucking stock which he contracted to furnish different rodeos as tho he went along himself. But he seldom did. Cal was getting old and he didn't care much for travelling any more. He'd done plenty of it during his race track days, for at one time he'd owned quite a string of race-horses, and raised many good ones, plenty good enough that they made him quite a stake. So that, with a few of his best horses he begin to cover more territory, taking in the bigger tracks, and his stake and winnings on his horses swelled up till he thought he was a sure enough race horse king.

And he was for a spell. Then his wife died while

bringing a daughter to the world. The daughter lived but right at the time she wasn't enough to fill the gap for the loss of the mother. She was placed in the best of care and Cal went on with his ponies, sort of wild and to higher stakes. He went to the top and stayed there for longer than was expected. Then the big stakes begin to fall, and as the pins begin to get knocked out from under him he played his ponies still higher, until one fine morning he found himself borrowing railroad fare to go back home with.

All the worth of his horses and stables had gone into turf dust.

But not his ranch, he'd kept that clean and sacred to the memory of his wife, and it would be kept so for their daughter's.

As the years went by, Cal contented himself with the ranch and to breeding up the few hundred cattle he had, also some good saddle and draft horses. No more racing stock for him. That had been a lot of fun and experience, and he'd found out that there was as much to learn in the race horse game as there is in the cattle game, that knowing and handling both well was too much for any one man. So, when the fun was over he was sort of glad of it in a way and so as to get back to his ranch and cattle. That was the game he was born and raised into and the one he really knew.

Busying himself as he had in having the whole ranch fixed up he didn't have no time to be lonesome nor grieve, and he often rode and worked along after his men had quit for the day. The old ranch had been much neglected during his horse racing spree, also much of his stock had strayed, and now that he had his little girl, Virginia, to do things for he'd set his whole heart to fix it all up as she and her mother would like it. That included the big ranch house and grounds surrounding first, then all other buildings, corrals and fences and the gathering in of the stock that had strayed.

As Virginia came to her fourth year, Cal got a good old fashioned lady ranch cook and house keeper, she was as good at fixing up homey medecines as she was at good food or even fancy puddings, and when the child came to the ranch she was so well taken care of, if not better, than at the special and expensive home where she'd been kept since infancy.

Cal had been mighty pleased at the natural way little Virginia took to the ranch. From the first day of her first summer there she acted like this wasn't at all new to her but very much at home, from the house to the corrals and horse pasture, and spread very much cheer over the whole outfit.

A couple of years later, Cal got Virginia a playmate of her choice to come and stay with her, also a tutor, and as she was very happy to stay at the ranch it also made Cal the same and much contented while she grew up there, most always in the open and often riding alongside of him.

Then there come another game to sort of draw Cal's attention. It was that of the rodeo, where cowboys contested and matched their skill against one another in bronco busting, steer roping and other range work in

arenas and for prizes. Cal didn't at first think such
doings would amount to much, but as years went by the
rodeos got more and more numerous and bigger right
along.

He sort of perked his ears at that, went to see a few
of the rodeos now and again and figured that there was
a real man's game, this one to be on the square, no doping
of stock and no buying of riders. He understood this
game, and when one day an old friend of the horse racing days drove in to the ranch to see him he'd got to
know some more of the rodeo and its doings, for that
old friend, after going busted on the fast horses, had
borrowed what money he could and invested it into the
rough ones, the kind that twisted up in the air in buck
jumps, landed hard and stayed pretty well in one spot
in trying to buck off their riders. They was plenty
speedy but not at all of the straight away kind.

He'd done fairly well in contracting to furnish them
horses for rodeos and paid off what he'd borrowed, then
he'd got some longhorn Mexico steers and bulls for the
wild steer riding and bull-dogging, and now he figured
he had about as good a string of rodeo stock as could
be gathered.

But he had no place of his own to keep them, and
that fall, after the rodeo season was over, he'd come to
see if Cal would winter 'em for him. Counting all, there'd
be about a hundred head.

Cal had always allowed plenty of range and stacked
feed for his stock, and consequences was he had it to
spare in case of long hard winters or droughts. Even

at that he didn't care to take on any more stock, but
for an old friend who was sort of under hard circum-
stances he agreed he would.

That's how come that some time later there come a
trailing the wildest looking bunch of horses and longhorns Cal had seen for a long time, and the riders who'd
trailed 'em up had been Brad, Jim and Red, as good a
cowboys as the stock was, plenty tough, and the same
boys who was now in the line camp, waiting for the
storm to ease up, and with practically the same stock.
Only a few had been replaced or added on.

This outlaw stock now belonged to Cal, had belonged
to him for some years, and the way that come about
wasn't thru any of Cal's choice of dickering. The stock
was sort of shoved onto him on account of his friend
taking sick, laying in the hospital for months and finally
dying. Having no one to care for him, Cal paid hospital,
doctor and burial fees, also what was still due on the
longhorns. And, with the ranging and feeding of the
stock, he didn't get it at no bargain. He done that only
for the sake of an old friend.

But he'd got himself some stock on his hands that'd
been easier to get than it was to be rid of and even tho
he'd lost his racing stock that had been a gamble he'd
more or less jumped into. But home at the ranch and
with regular stock dealings he wasn't the one to sacrifice
and sell at a loss. He wouldn't have the big ranch if
he had.

Knowing that he couldn't sell the horses as work stock
and the wiry longhorns as beef cattle and get anywheres

near the amount he'd put out on 'em he'd advertised 'em
for sale in many western newspapers from border to
border, and as stock for rodeo purposes, which they sure
enough was.

Only a few nibbles came from that, none worth considering. He kept the horses for over a year without
any use of 'em, when they only accumulated more fat
and meanness, if that was possible.

Then, being he'd kept Brad and the other two boys
to ride on the ranch when not following the rodeos, it
came to him that he himself could promote contracts
for the use of them in rodeos. Them three boys could
well handle the shipping and care of the stock for him
for whatever rodeo he might contract with. Besides, the
boys could dig up and arrange some more contracts,
to his approval, and that way he would at least get some
returns from what he'd put in that stock.

Talking it over with the boys it was more than agreeable with 'em, and besides getting regular wages right
along they would also get a percentage on every contract that Cal agreed to. It was also agreed that Brad,
on account of being more out to contesting than either
Jim or Red, was appointed chief and would have full
charge of the stock. All three would be allowed to attend
any rodeo at any time wether Cal's stock would be used
at such rodeos or not, but would need to be at the ranch
for regular cow work and horse breaking when not busy
at contesting. That was all agreeable too.

If he'd looked the country over, Cal couldn't got
better agents and handlers for his stock for the rodeo

game. They knew the ropes of that game, they was well liked, and being they contested in other rodeos besides where Cal's stock was contracted and played no favorites as to judges all went well.

The first year, and without an extra worry or move on his part, Cal netted enough to fill quite a hole in what he'd been out on the stock. The following year was still better, and then's when he decided to keep that bunch of outlaws, for beside being profitable they kind of kept his blood a tingling in hearing of how hard his horses was to set and his longhorns to ride, rope and bull-dog. He got to have his favorites amongst the outlaws the same as he had with his race stock. And even tho there was no betting, when his buckers came back after a summer's round of rodeos and a few of his top ones hadn't been stuck to or qualified on by some of the best riders, he felt about the same thrill as when one of his thoroughbreds came in the money.

Another thing, with that string, was that when some of the horses he'd raise and would have broke was inclined to turn to the bad he'd just turn 'em in along with the buckers and have 'em make the rounds of the rodeos till that was out of their system. If they didn't quit, well and good, so long as they could buck hard enough. If not they could then easy be sold as broke, at least from bucking, and without a bit of harm to their spirit, for none of 'em was *made* to buck and none was abused in keeping them from it.

Sometimes even some of the old buckers would quit, and them that had been good and a long time at the game was pensioned to spend the rest of their lives in

idleness and right along with the good faithful old cowhorses, on good feed, shade and shelter. There was always plenty of young stock to take the place of the bad
as well as the good and both kinds was given every
chance to be either, according to their nature.

In the line camp and switching from the talk on the
colt to the prospects for the coming winter, the boys
then begin to reminisce some on the past years and when
they'd first took on the handling of Cal's rodeo stock,
and summing it all up, as they had time and again before, they figured they was riding pretty (doing very
well) as compared to most other cowboys who followed
the contests. They had a place to come to whenever they
was thru and their wages and work going on just the
same they never was broke, all outside of Red who was
bound to draw ahead on his wages every once in a while.
Jim had a failing for fancy silver-mounted riggings
but he managed to save some of his money, sometimes
for more. As for Brad having no fault excepting of
shooting out bright lights now and again on account,
as he'd say "they hurt his eyes," had saved quite a stake
in spite of having to pay for many lights and fines, and
cartridges.

And with all the remeniscing it would always come
to them, as it did now, that after all the excitement,
thrills and spills and rodeos was over how sort of glad
and relieved they felt to come back to the ranch and
rest up with just plain hard range work. It was like
their home only they felt more free, and that's the cowboy's big weakness, to be free.

The cabin getting chilly the while they talked, one of the boys went to look at the fire. It had burned out, had been out for quite a while, and surprised that it wasn't so cold he opened the door to look outside. It had quit snowing but the wind was still blowing as strong as ever, only now from another direction and warm, so warm that after the cold of not long before it near felt hot. It was the chinook Brad had figured would come.

At the sound of "chinook" all three went outside. It was good the storm was over, over at least for the time, and knowing that a storm often follows a chinook they figured that now they could get to the ranch before that other storm would come.

With the warm wind the snow had quit drifting, it was now packing, melting and crumbling in layers as the wind cut thru the drifts like a knife, and from under them little streams started to run, run on ground that was now bare of the inches of snow that had covered it only an hour or so before.

Looking down towards the creek bottom and breaks where the horses had hit for shelter during the storm it was seen that they'd now come out and was grazing on higher and open land. The sight of them reminded Brad of Roper and the colt which he'd left in the shelter of the cabin, and now, even before getting to the corner to look around and see if they was still there he knew they wouldn't be. And they wasn't, for they'd also went on to feed and maybe was now amongst the other horses.

"Afoot, I see." Red grinned at him. "Better get your

baby in before this wind switches and brings on another blizzard or he'll sure turn into a statue."

It had got late in the afternoon, too late so it'd be of any advantage to start out with the horses. If the chinook kept up during the night, or even only part of it, the snow would be most all gone. And maybe turning some colder by morning the ground wouldn't be so slushy and the going would then be easier.

They would get an early start on the next morning, Brad said, and get to the ranch in good time that afternoon.

That settled, and the wood pile now bared of snow and in plain sight, Red went to work on cutting and chopping some of it, enough to do for the rest of that day and for the night, also enough for the boys who'd be coming along with the cattle, for travelling slower and making another camp they wouldn't get to the line camp until the next day, and being it's the custom in the cow-country that wood burned should always be replaced for the next traveller, Red started in on the job. Jim would relay on him sometime but right then the stove and what should be fixed for supper seemed to take a lot of his attention.

While that was going on, Brad edged away, and Red watching him from the corner of his eye let him go for a ways, then hollered.

"Just look for a horse blanket," he grinned, "then look under it and there he'll be."

Brad walked on towards the grazing horses. It was easy to pick out the outlaws from the used saddle horses, for at the sight of him they begin to spook and run in a big circle around him, heads up and a snorting, while the saddle horses stood still and just looked or grazed. Neither the colt nor Roper was among them but was soon located off a ways, the both of 'em grazing side by side.

Thru a patch of aspens, Brad came closer to them without being seen, and coming to a bare ledge of rock he sat down, rolled a cigarette and, for nothing else to do, watched 'em.

He watched as the colt, his head close to Roper's, was grazing in the same spots Roper would paw the snow off for the good grass underneath, better grass than where it was more open and the chinook had bared of snow.

Brad had to grin some as the colt followed Roper step by step and even tried to root him out of the grass he'd bared. He'd follow him from patch to patch then watch him paw, curious as any kid watching a grown up cracking nuts and as ready to pounce on the meat as any kid would. But all this watching wasn't for pure curiosity, it was also for learning, and at one time, when Roper wouldn't be rooted away Brad was surprised to see the colt go to one side a few feet and with his small hoofs paw up his own grass.

As he watched, Brad seen that he'd do that near every time Roper wouldn't let him in on what he'd dug up, and at that he had to grin some more.

"Learning pretty fast, young feller," he says, half aloud. "Didn't think that with the hundreds of years of high breeding and man's steady care you'd keep the instinct of rustling your own food. But I'm thinking that out here there'll be other instincts come back to you which has long been asleep in the blood of your past generations."

The lids of the little tin stove was rattling long before daybreak the next morning as the boys got up and made ready for an early start. Breakfast was soon cooked and over with and then the coffee pot made its usual rounds, dishes and camp cleaned up, and after a few more cigarettes it was light enough so the horses could be corralled.

To see the colt go to one side a few feet and with his small
hoofs paw up his own grass

A fresh horse fed grain and kept up for the night was soon saddled and Jim rode out to bring in the saddle horses, and when a short time later they was corralled, Brad seen that the colt was right there among 'em. It had been his first night in the open western country, and it being warm, he seemed to've done well. It'd turn considerable cooler during morning, but the wind had died down and now the colt's blanket was pulled off. A little feed of grain while the buckers was being gathered and brought up and he was ready for travel.

As the boys had figured, the travelling was much better than it would have been the evening before. The snow, all but a few scattering banks was gone, the water had run off the now bare earth and when the horses was all bunched and started out they took to the open in good shape, the colt right by Roper, and now that he'd had a good rest, feed and water and wasn't hindered by the blanket he went along like a good one. There was no deep snow nor strong, cold wind to buck against now, and at the start he'd been good for a run if the others would only start one.

But he sort of got over that after a time, and did as the other horses did, trot or walk along, stop for a few bites of bunch grass and trot and walk along some more as the bunch was steady being drove on.

It got warmer along towards noon, and under a chinooky sky, no sun, the ground got a little heavy to travel on in some places. There was a stop made by a deep creek where the horses drank and grazed for a spell. The boys just "rested their saddles," meaning they got off their horses, hobbled 'em and let 'em graze while they, themselves, just sat on a dead tree and smoked. There was no lunch brought along, for like with most cowboys, such is seldom thought of.

In good time the bunch was again started on the way, now on the home stretch and there'd be no more stops. Over foothill ridges, acrost steep coulees and ravines then rolling land the bunch trailed along steady, and once again, during middle afternoon, the colt begin to get tired and to lagging behind Roper more and more.

Noticing that, Red remarked to Brad, "Looks like your urchin is going to quit again. Better ride on ahead to the ranch and get a team and wagon to take him in, and some more blankets too for the poor thing."

Brad only grinned at the joking remark, for the colt was doing fairly well and still would for quite a ways. He did, but when finally the bunch was drove over a low pass and down a fair sized valley pretty well surrounded by tall mountains, the colt's legs begin to get pretty wobblely and he was going mostly on his nerve and sense of having to go on the rest of the way in. He didn't see the long spread of corrals, sheds and building which now wasn't so far in the distance, and when finally he followed the bunch of horses into one of the corrals he hardly noticed 'em nor even the dry and warm stable Brad right away helped him into. Once inside he just slowly layed down on some dry waste hay, closed his eyes, and drew a long relaxing breath which all went as much as to say, "This must be home."

CHAPTER FOUR

HOME ON THE RANGE

AS comfortable as the colt was made in the long log stable and in the company of other horses which he heard munching hay in their stalls, the boys in the bunk house was also as comfortable, for after a good warm supper then back into their own beds there was no more thought of the steam-heated hotel rooms.

The night went by like in no time, a good breakfast spread out by the ranch cook which was nicknamed "Grouch" on account he was just the opposite, and then, as the boys went back to the bunk house for a smoke, Old Cal came to join 'em there, to sort of resume his welcome of the evening before.

Brad was the first one he picked on and putting his hand out to him, he smiled and says "I'm mighty proud of you, my boy, for bringing home the honor of three first prizes for bronc riding this year. I sure want to congratulate you."

"Thanks," says Brad who wasn't much at taking compliments. "But I most likely wouldn't come back with any of the three prizes if I'd been riding the tops of *your* string, Cal. The last contest was the only time where I won first on one of yours. It was that loose jointed blue roan called Thunderhead and he's not one of your hardest to set, even if he does put on a good show."

It was that loose jointed blue roan called Thunderhead and he's not one of your hardest to set

"Yes," says Cal, sticking up for both Brad and the horse, "and he's bucked off some mighty good riders just the same."

So saying, he layed some newspapers and clippings on the table telling of Brad's good riding and winnings; then he turned to Jim and Red. "You two boys didn't do so doggone bad either, and I'm also very proud of you, very pleased with the good contracts too, and the way my stock was handled by you and Brad all the way thru."

"We sure done our best," says Red, "and now don't blame me nor Jim for the addition to the stock."

"Addition! What addition?" asks Cal, looking at one after another of the boys.

"Ain't you seen it yet?" Red grinned. "It's in one of the empty stud's box stalls, and for all I think it amounts to the stall is still empty."

Not at all bothered at Red's remarks, Brad put on his coat and, starting for the door, says. "Come on, Cal, I'll show 'it' to you, as Red calls him."

In the stable, and as the colt raised his head from the filled manger to blink at the two men, Cal also done some blinking. Brad led the colt out of the stall, and without saying a word, Cal walked all around him observing every point. Finally, and without taking his eyes from the colt, he says:

"Why, this is a hot blood all the way thru or I've never seen one." Then he asked, "Where and how did you get him?"

"Just picked him up at the yards where we shipped from after the last rodeo."

Cal rubbed his chin a bit. "Kind of queer," he says. Then he asked. "Know anything about him?"

"Some," says Brad. "Plenty enough to satisfy me."

"Well, that ought to be enough. But now, what do you aim to do with him?"

"Thought I'd give him to Virginia. Maybe she'd like him to train and for a sort of a pet."

That last came pretty well of a sudden, and Brad surprised himself even as he spoke. For, ever since he'd seen the colt he'd wondered what had prompted him to buy him. As for a rope horse he knew that he wasn't of the breed nor built that would do, and he'd used that only as an excuse, to himself as well as others. Another excuse, which would have been enough by itself, was that he'd took a liking to the colt. But with that, and not wanting to admit it even to himself was thoughts of Virginia, that she would like him.

And now that he'd blurted it out, like as much as to say the colt was a present to her, there was no taking it back and he was near as surprised in what he'd just said as Cal was of hearing it.

Cal rubbed his chin some more, and squinting at Brad, he says, "Mighty fine of you, my boy, and I know Virginia will sure be tickled witless. But," he hesitated some. "But, daggone it, Brad I was thru with racing stock. Had enough of 'em long ago. Lost 'em all about sixteen years ago, when Virginia was three years old."

Brad stood mighty silent, not knowing what to say or do. For one thing he hadn't meant to come right out and say the colt was for Virginia, and another was he didn't know of Cal's stand on thoroughbreds. But it was said and done and over with now. And maybe it was just as well, or better, that way.

Cal walked to the stable door, looked outside a while, and then turned to Brad who was still standing and just looking at the colt.

"Well—" he says. "What're you standing there for. Why don't you go up to the house and tell her?"

"Guess I won't now," says Brad. "Didn't know of your dealings with thoroughbreds and that you was thru with 'em."

Old Cal sort of melted at that. "Don't take me wrong there, Brad," he says. "This just got me kind of sudden and I spoke before I thought. I ain't got nothing against thoroughbreds, and even if I'm thru with 'em one sure won't hurt, not at all, when considering how happy Virginia would be in having him. We'll wait and see what she says."

They didn't have to wait long, for as the two talked and Brad was currying and brushing the colt there come a shadow at the stable door and where Cal had been standing just few minutes before. It was the slender figure of Virginia herself, and as Cal had blinked in surprise at the sight of the colt so did she, and so was Cal and Brad right then, blinking at her.

She didn't seem to see neither of them as she walked to the colt, and she'd never seen thoroughbreds before only in pictures. But at the sight of the colt she recognized him as one right away and just had to touch him to see if he was real. Finally after feeling of his smooth

There come a shadow at the stable door

thin hide along his slim neck and head, then his long fine-boned legs she looked at her dad, and some excited, she asked her dad:

"Where does he come from? Whose is he?"

Old Cal, grinning at her excitement, waved a hand towards Brad. "Ask him," he says.

She then looked at Brad for an answer and, "If you really want to know," he says, "you've first got to tell me what you think of him."

The girl was kind of stumped at that, and as she stroked the colt's fine mane, she was, for the time, plum against it as to what to say. And seeing her predicament, also sort of sensing what she wanted to say, Brad went on.

"Well," he grinned. "He's from the blue grass country, and as to whose he is, he's yours, if you want him."

The girl was now more stumped than before. She looked straight at Brad, like to make sure he meant it, then to her dad, and finally managed to say:

"Oh, dad, is it true? Can I really have him?"

Old Cal, now looking puzzled, only shrugged his shoulders and once more waved his hand toward Brad, not saying a word.

Virginia was now sure, and in the wink of an eye had her arms around her dad's neck and kissed him. She also got Brad about as quick. That clinched the deal, and he didn't try to duck and when the two come to, one was again mixed up with a thoroughbred and the other was without that horse.

Now that the colt had changed hands it didn't take long for the new owner to take charge of him. Brad handed her the halter rope, the curry comb and brush, and grinning at Cal, throwed up his hands. Cal answered with another shrug, and being they now seen they was plum forgotten, walked out of the stable.

During that day and the next the boys was busy doing nothing much but straightening their personal stuff what had been brought from the railroad station, also getting an idea on what all was to be done in the line of work which Cal always saved as much of as could for whenever they'd return there, and he usually had a lot of it stacked up, some of it which should of been done before but couldn't without their help. Such as with all range work, rounding up, branding, moving the stock to different winter quarters, shipping of beef cattle and all such.

The longhorn herd of steers and bulls came trailing in a couple of days later and them was put in special tight pasture of good grass and shelter, and by long sheds for feeding during storms was stacks of hay.

While the boys would be gone on their rounds of rodeos off and on during summers, Cal kept only one rider on the job. With him and himself, and then the boys drifting in for sometimes a couple of weeks and pitching in on the riding it was pretty well kept up. Also, being that less riding was needed to be done during them months and some could be held off it worked well for when the boys would drift in to stay as late fall would come, for fall and spring was the most rushing times and when more riders would be needed. Brad would be about the only one who'd be apt to break loose most any time, but with making his winnings and connecting for contracts for Cal's stock at coming rodeos he much more than earned his goings.

With the two riders who'd trailed in the longhorns, and Cal as the boss that made seven men to go on the fall works which would keep them all busy until winter set in. By then it would or should be done and only about three riders would be needed after that, also about the same amount of the ranch hands to feed the hay them same hands had stacked the summer before.

For the need of fresh and more saddle horses, the

horse round up was first, and being that none excepting
a few renegades ranged over a day's ride from the ranch,
Virginia was now on hand at that most every day, and
later on with the cattle round up, until the circles got too
far for her to make and still be able to be back to the
ranch when night come. For a cow camp is no place for
a lady, and as welcome as one is, it put the boys out, in
many ways, like with their appearance and language,
and especially when needing some indoor heat after long
days of riding in the cold, windy and snowy spells that
come in the fall.

Realizing that very well, Virginia was then contented
to riding within easy distance of the ranch. For now,
along with the riding to be done close to the ranch while
they was away, her work and other interests in the house,
there was the colt which drawed much of her attention
and spent most of her spare time with.

Virginia, after some long winters at college, would now
be spending the coming one, the first one in years, at
home, at the ranch. She'd figured she had plenty of education to do her, and Cal, missing her more than anyone
but himself ever knew while she was away, more than
agreed with her.

"Enough of anything is aplenty," he'd said, "and now
that you're going on nineteen, a little more outside education sure won't hurt you none. Not that you're not
already well elucated that way, but I've had over forty
years of it and every day I learn something to the good
that shows me how little I know as compared to what
all there is to know.

"It's the way in most everything, I guess, but the outside learning is a heap more healthful and interesting, I think."

With the coming winter, the colt would be a lot of added pleasure and company to her. She would care and train him so he would grow to be a fine horse. As for what purpose she didn't know as yet. She knew some that his breed wasn't much good for anything but racing and she didn't know how she could have use for any such.

But time would tell, and now an important thing was to give him a name, a name that would fit him during his colthood as well as it would when he grew up. It should be a sort of high sounding name and fitting to his breed. Then, thinking of the country he was from, and the way it had struck her while at college, how many persons of high standing was called Colonel in that country more than in any other, she figured that would identify him as to his country, also as to a good standing. She liked the name too, once she thought of it, and that's how come the little thoroughbred was named Colonel, Colonel to stay.

The weather had been good, near like Indian summer, since the few days of storm that'd come when the bucking stock had been trailed home. The colt, Colonel, was now turned outside in a big corral most every day, one adjoining another corrall which was for feeding and where from a few to many horses was kept right long. With that company to rub nostrils thru the corral bars, the sun and the big space to play in he come right to in good shape and got well weaned away from his home pastures, even his mother.

The long trip and distance had a lot to do with that weaning, then the trailing to the ranch added on till now it didn't matter to him much where he was. It of course helped some when Brad would come near, for he'd got to know him, and somehow as a good friend in connection to getting him away from that dark damp stall of the stock yards to the east. Then there was the big gray outlaw which he'd got some comfort in being near to during the trip, then Roper during the trailing on in.

Now, Virginia was first up in his mind. She was the one who early in the morning fed him his grain, groomed and scratched him while he et, then led him out into the big corral to where a stream from a warm spring which run the winter thru came under the bars into one corner of the corral. In the center was a manger where she'd put in a forkful of special good hay, clover and alfalfa mixed. But before going to that, and soon as he got thru drinking and was turned loose, the colt would have to have his roll, and a good one. It was a luxury he wouldn't of had at his home paddocks, not after a grooming such as the girl would give him. But she would just smile and enjoyed watching him as much as the colt enjoyed rolling, for that was more satisfying and natural than the grooming.

Then one day, after the beef cattle was gathered to be trailed in and shipped and the whole outfit came in to the ranch for one night stay, there was amongst the saddle horses one very poor little colt of only a couple of months old which Virginia, who'd rode out to meet the herd, at once spotted.

Brad had found him some days before, all alone and just sort of moping along like hardly knowing where he was going, weak and wobbling from thirst and hunger, for the colt was still too young to get along without his mother. It was figured that as there was a few bunches of wild horses in that country the colt was one of 'em and had been left behind during a chase by some wild horse runners. He'd been too young to keep up and it was a wonder the cayotes hadn't got him.

There sure was no wildness about him that day when Brad rode up close, only just enough life, life to realize there was a horse near him and not at all caring about the rider sitting on that horse. For, to his instinct, horse-flesh meant life, such as his mother had given him.

With a weak little nicker he'd raised his head at the nearness of the horse he could hardly see, and the way he tried to show how pleased he was was sort of pitiful in the thought of the suffering that little feller had gone thru.

At a glance of him, Brad knew there was only two things to do. He seen that the colt couldn't make it to camp on his shaky legs, he would have to be carted in and taken care of. The only other thing to do would be to shoot him and save him from slow suffering to death. Then he thought of Colonel at the ranch and the good company this little feller would be for him during the winter, if he could be got there, made to live and get his strength again.

With that in mind, Brad finished the circle (ride) he'd set out to make, and back to camp he got some of the

There was a few bunches of wild horses in that country the colt was one of 'em
and had been left behind during a chase

boys to help him unload what grub there was in the one wagon (it was no regular chuck wagon as there was was with the big outfits), a team was harnessed and hooked to it, Red jumped in with Brad and the two drove acrost quite a few miles of rough country to as close to the colt as they could get. Then taking one of the horses from the wagon they easy enough got up to him, when he followed the horse back to the wagon, where he was soon caught and loaded.

With diluted and warmed canned milk gradually poured down the colt's throat once in a while he seemed to revive some and getting strength. Bunch grass was even pulled and brought to him but he was still too young to any more than nibble at that. When the beef was gathered and the outfit started back for the ranch, room was made for him in the wagon, up to within a few miles of the ranch, then he was turned loose to go with the saddle horses the rest of the way.

A little later, when Virginia rode up to the saddle horse bunch and, Red who'd been driving them, seeing her looking at the colt in wonder, had to laugh some.

"Yep," he says riding nearer. "It's another one of Brad's thoroughbreds, only this one is not from the blue grass country, he's from the sage brush and badland hills. But he's a sure enough thoroughbred just the same, a thoroughbred little wild horse. He don't look it now, does he? But the poor little feller sure aint had no chance."

Virginia gave him the chance. In the same corral with Colonel where there was the warm water and choice hay, warm milk and a mush of ground barley fed him every once in a while, laying in the sun during the day and in a warm stable during the night, no more exhausting himself roaming the country, looking for his mother or the water to quench his thirst, it was less than a week when he begin to be up and a coming. As close as he'd been to going to horse heaven the hardiness of the wild horse, along with Virginia's good care, had pulled him thru.

With the two colts now and the care Virginia gave them, that turned out to be quite a chore, a chore to the girl's own doing and liking, and there was few days when she wasn't with 'em for long spells at a time, even during stormy weather, for if not in the stable there was always some sheltered spots amongst the windbreaks of the sheds and many corrals, and the colts got their daily exercise wether it snowed, rained or the sun shined.

It was with great interest that the girl watched the little wild colt steady gaining strength, and a sort of rewarding surprise when one day, as she turned him out in the big corral, she seen him start to run, let out a squeal and like he wanted to play. Colonel, far from having been neglected on account of the newcomer and now being full of vigor, seemed as surprised at the colt's first sign of play as the girl was, and like for encouragement went to running circles around him and to cutting some capers in trying to egg him on.

It had been quite some puzzle to Colonel that day past when the little shrunk up and starving wild colt was half carried and pulled in by Red and Virginia, to be layed close to the sunny side of the corral. At first he'd been half scared of the little feller, like it is with all horses, to sense and keep shy of any dying or dead animal, and he wouldn't come near unless Virginia was there while caring for him, then it'd only be to take a sniff, at a safe distance.

It wasn't until the colt started to walk around some that he begin to prance around him and showing off, and even tho the sick little feller would only stand and watch at such goings on it sort of helped him with wanting to do the same, like he had at one time while he was with his mammy. He'd been a speedy one then too, but with all the suffering he'd gone thru that seemed a long time past and near forgotten. Colonel's acting up was good medicine towards making him remember.

But even during his sick and recuperative spell, the little colt was good if not lively company to Colonel, and after the dangerous time was over and his first step faster than a walk was made, his strength, thru Virginia's steady care, came fast and surprising. So, well and out of danger finally, Virginia begin to think of a fitting name for him too, a name fitting the breed of his ancestors or suggesting of their country, the same as she had with Colonel.

Thinking of such a breed the name would have to be Spanish, for the Spaniards having brought the first horses to America some few hundreds years before, and this little feller being a descendant of them same horses, which had accumulated, spread over the whole Southwest and gone wild as antelope, he should be named according.

Virginia thought of many Spanish names, long and short, and not knowing as yet of what he'd turn out to be she went on taking a chance, hoping he'd some day be as good a horse as a man had to be to be entitled to such a name as she decided on. She called him "Charro," meaning top cowboy of the better class, and sort of Jim Dandy.

His color was now a dark mouse color but looking at the base of his ears, back of his elbows and at his flanks, the girl figured that when spring come and he done his first shedding he'd turn out to be a "grulla" (pronounced gruya) which is also a Spanish name. Virginia thought some of giving him that name, but she didn't like it quite well enough, and the color itself wouldn't be pretty. It's what's called a dirty gray, a mixture of iron gray and roan and sort of rusty. But the color is not what makes the horse, and knowing that very well, Virginia figured she'd make up by name what he lacked in color, and she'd see to it he'd have every chance to be a good horse.

The winter set in and wore on with all going well, regardless of the tough weather that came. The colts getting the best of care, fed picked hay, right amounts of crushed barley and warm spring water to drink from when they wished, got to playing and acting up so that as Virginia would sometimes watch 'em, she wondered if the eight foot corral fence would be tall enough to hold 'em. But neither was of the high-jumping breed, and even tho they had good runs at it, the corral being big and roomy enough so it had often held a thousand cattle, with plenty of space for a thousand more, they always came to a slide or fast turn when the tall pole fence loomed up in front of 'em.

In their play, feeding and resting, there was nothing come to disturb or stop 'em from any growth. All was to their advantage, and even tho Charro had growed more middle on him than he should have, making him look sort of puny at both ends, that was to be expected with any colt when losing their mother too soon. Even the good care he'd got that couldn't of been helped, but that out of proportion middle didn't seem to at all bother his action once he got his strength, and when spring with green grass and clover would come he would soon enough lose that thick middle and get to regular shape.

All went also well in general with the Hip O ranch and range. There was plenty of stacked and standing feel for all stock, snows came at right amounts and time to insure good moisture for the following spring and summer, and all hands was at their regular winter camps doing their regular work.

Brad and Red was kept at the ranch most of the time on account they might hit out most any day and cross the mountains to do some contesting that would be pulled off along the Coast. Jim, not being inclined that way, was at one of the winter camps, where him and a couple of ranch hands batched and where over half of the Hip O cattle was being kept track of and wintered. The other riders, outside of the one which was kept on steady and was now at another winter camp, was let go.

With Brad and Red there wasn't so much for them to

do, only lining out (breaking) a few colts while keeping tab on the strong cattle that was wintering on the range and now and again bringing in few that would need feeding, the feeding being done by the ranch hands. The bucking horses was also fed some, but with the well shel-tered pasture they was in and the good standing feed that was there was the pawing, they seldom touched the hay that was spread out for them. They kept fat, wild and snorty.

It was about the same with the longhorn steers and bulls, and even tho they did take on more hay than the horses did on account cattle don't paw for their feed as horses do, they only looked wild eyed at the ranch hands that fed 'em, and the shaking of their threatening long horns as a warning they'd better stay on their hay rack, was the only thanks them boys would get.

Along about middle winter there come a notice of a good rodeo being pulled off away to the south and west. There would be quite a few following from then on, and Brad slipped on his best boots, took his pet spurs and away he went. He done well down there in the warm climes, so well that Red soon joined him, and now Cal was without any riders but himself at the ranch. But as that had been expected he soon had one good one, one who had no rodeo ambition, to take their place until they returned. Then that rider would still be kept on the job, for by that time the spring works would be starting.

CHAPTER FIVE

THE VERY WIDE AND OPEN SPACES

OLD man winter, after covering the land with a good blanket of snow, kept his grip on a cold that averaged from zero to ten below, and a few days when it skidded down to forty and then fifty below. There was no thawing nor warm spells, and that was good, for the stock being hardened to the cold would of only weakened from the warm spells and suffered more when cold weather would come on again.

As it was and the way it stayed cold well over the season, when spring did come there was no doubt about it. It came gradual and as every living thing would wish it, and when one fine early morning a meadow lark lit on a branch not far from Viriginia's half-opened window and sang to a tune that could of well been understood as "Why girl, you're sleeping your life away," that girl of a sudden woke and sat up in bed to more appreciate the song. It was the first meadow lark she'd heard that spring and it created a great feeling to listen to it, like one being freed from old man winter's grip, and warm breezes and green lands was ahead.

But the meadow lark had to take on some more chilly weather after announcing that "spring is here," and it was many more days before patches of bare ground begin to show, and much longer before the frost got out of the ground and the grass begin to warm up to the heat of the sun.

Finally there come a time when, as the colts was turned out into the big corral and went to limbering up with their usual play, that they would now and again stop, sniff high at the air and then look thru the bars at the country around. It was getting green and the smell of the thawing earth and sprouting grass in the air is what they was filling their nostrils and lungs with.

With that they begin to lose their taste for hay, and even the crushed barley which now contained some conditioning powders was hardly eaten. Virginia well understood what was ailing them, it was their craving for the green grass they could smell and see, and they made it mighty hard on her for not letting them out to it. They wouldn't follow her around so much no more, and as she'd sometimes talk to 'em their sense of hearing was more with their sense of smelling and they'd be more apt to be looking thru the bars at the greening meadows than be cocking an ear to her. She would laugh a little then and tell them that she would turn them loose soon, soon as the grass was of good enough length so they wouldn't starve nor wear themselves down in trying to get a few nips of it. For she knew that once they got a taste of the green grass they wouldn't touch their hay no more unless starved to it, nor hardly the grain, and the grass they could get wouldn't be near enough to do 'em, not for a while yet. It all depended on the fairy of spring, now that old man winter had gone.

Charro, coming alongside, didn't wait quite so long

Then, like as tho the fairy took pity on Virginia, who felt so sorry for the colts wanting to get out as much as she wanted to let 'em and couldn't, it seemed like the land turned green with grass popping up over night, as by magic from the fairy's wand.

A few warm nights and days when the snow line got higher up the tall mountains and all begin to grow and bud, and then one fine morning as the meadow larks sang to the tune "It's high time to be out now," Virginia went down to the big corral where the colts had passed the long winter and opened one big gate wide.

The colts just stood and blinked at the wide opening of the gate for a spell, like a blindfold had just been lifted off their eyes. Colonel came to the girl, nudged her with his nose, then looked past her as much as to ask and make sure if it was true, this wide opening to the green pasture.

Charro, coming alongside, didn't wait quite so long. The green grass which he'd been born too late in the year to taste drawed him now as natural as the warm sun drawed the grass itself, and he took the lead out to it. Colonel followed then, and once thru the gate and out in the big pasture he was at first for kicking up his heels and having a good run, but soon as he put his nose down to earth and got a whiff of the green grass that stopped him as tho he'd of a sudden took root right there. It had been the same with Charro, and now the two went to enjoying the first blades of green like they'd never enjoyed anything so before.

Virginia, watching 'em, was also having as much enjoyment in doing just that as the colts was with their grazing. Perching herself on top of the high corral fence, her back to the warm sun, she watched 'em for near an hour, and during that time a few of Cal's top horses, including a couple of Virginia's, trotted up to see what the newcomers was.

There was some pleasant excitement as the colts and grown ups met, and for the time the grazing was forgotten as all went to running and playing which was part of getting acquainted, and finally getting out of sight beyond willow thickets as they played and run, Virginia got down from the corral, went into the stable, saddled one of her horses which she'd kept up and rode away from the ranch towards the center of the big valley. For she also wanted to enjoy the spring air and sun.

To make the riding more interesting (she never went out for idle riding) there was work to be done which was much to her liking and fitted well with that time of the year. As she got further down the valley and thru sunny openings amongst willow and cottonwood groves, little white faced calves begin to jump up and scamper away from where they'd been sunning themselves. The youngest would only raise up, blink at her, stand and watch her ride by, some so curious they would follow for a ways. Then there was others, a day or two old, which hid by their mothers, would flatten to the ground at the sound of her horse's hoofs as she came near and wouldn't even wiggle an ear if she rode by.

Them hiding little fellers was the ones that caused most of her work, for if she didn't find the calf and then rode onto a cow that looked like she'd had one it would mean that the calf should be hunted up and found because, as sometimes happens, a calf is born in places where he can't get up, like maybe at the edge of a hollow he might fall backwards into it while scrambling to get on his feet, then again where brush, rocks or dirt back will keep him from getting his legs under so's to get up. Some fool cows will even have their calves in a pool of water which might freeze during the night, and other such ways where a calf never lives to get the first nursing which would give him strength.

Knowing cattle well, and seeing a cow that'd calved not long before, without the calf by her side, was when Virginia would start hunting for it. It's most always the case that the cow just hides the calf while she goes grazing, and as the range cow is always watchful of any rider or anything coming near her calf she'll run to where she hid it and there to stand guard, and in doing that, giving away her calf's hiding place.

But some cows are wise, and instead of doing that will lead the rider plum away from where the calf has been hid. Then's when the hunting would be hard and the work, or sometimes fun for her, would come in.

There was more than a couple of hundred head in the herd which Virginia was keeping an eye on. These was cows that was to have earlier calves than the others and had been cut out and kept close to the ranch for the care some of 'em would need.

In riding thru and tallying up on the herd every day, there was more than the little calves to watch out for.

The mothers, even tho strong as they might be, would
sometimes get down, and like with some of the critters,
in the worst places they could find, as tho they wanted to
commit suicide. Most of that work she could handle with
the help of her good saddlehorse and her rope, and it was
seldom she'd need any help from other riders or ranch
hands.

With that responsible work and other riding which
followed on and which she liked so, her interest with the
colts, her picked saddle horses and other stock she kept
pretty happily busy outside. Then there was the inside
too, in the big ranch house, and with the cheerful company of faithful Anne who'd about taken a mother's
place in her affections, she chatted while sometimes help-
ing her with the house work, arranging it, sewing and
then with some of the mysteries of cooking, reading of
evenings with the company of her dad, and Anne who'd
sit with 'em for a while, especially when the radio came,
all filled Virginia's days to the brim with everything
she hankered for. She was free to do as she pleased and
for that she was very pleased with just what she was
doing.

Once in a while some of her college friends would
come to the ranch and visit with her, sometimes taking
her back with them when there was some special doings
or party she wanted to attend or maybe some shopping
to do. There was a few sprouts and older gents on her
trail, but none seemed to make her heart flutter any.
And as far as her future, which she seldom thought of
on account it was just fine the way it was, assured and

peaceful. And to her, the ranch, the range, horses and cattle was what she'd never dream of wanting to get away from.

With the coming of spring, Brad and Red come a straggling into the ranch after their rounds at contesting, a little the worse for wear but well satisfied with most all they done. It was good to be "home" again to rest up with the steady goings on and work where they'd left off three months or so before. The four year old colts they'd started to break was run in again, and now turning five would be more mature and could stand more riding.

Bunches of horses was run in and them colts was kept back, along with new ones to start on, from three to five year olds. There was no older unbroke geldings on the Hip O, for there was steady use for them, good or bad.

With the first handling of these wild and strong broncs (unbroke or outlaw range horses), Virginia was often in the corral and watching Brad and Red saddle and ride the snorty ones, some times for so long that she'd have to ride hard so's to catch up with her work in tallying up on the cows and calves, and sometimes too, one or both of the boys would ride out with her and help, which was good work in the breaking of the broncs.

There was a spell then when the little fellers, Colonel and Charro, was also some neglected. But they sure didn't need no more care now, and even tho they'd come to meet her when she came in the pasture it was more to be doing something and like saying hallo to one who'd been such a good friend to them during the winter. But

even tho they wouldn't have cared much for grain, much
less hay and couldn't be attracted that way, there was
one more way. They was fast shedding now and their
hides was mighty itchy, especially Charro's whose hair,
on account of the hardship he'd gone thru in losing
his mother while so young, was coming out in patches.

Then's when Virginia came along with a curry comb
and stiff brush and gave each good going overs. Right
then that beat any of whatever else she might of given
'em. She would spend quite a bit of time doing that most
every day, and when in a couple of weeks' time they got
slick and shiny and no more winter hair was left, they
still hankered for more scratching, because then the flies
begin to come, from the near invisible nose flies to the
big black "bulldogs" which would light on top center
of a horse's rump, where he could hardly get at 'em,
and often draw blood. There is other parts where swarms
of stinging little flies keep a coming to as fast as a horse
can swish 'em away and sometimes make a long raw sore,
that's back of the front legs, along the center of the
belly.

The colts being pestered with most all kinds of flies
that way would now more than welcome the sight of Virginia coming in the pasture during the long evenings.
They'd break into a lope to meet her then, crowd her
and one another to be the first and get the most scratching, and being the little wild colt, Charro, was now as
tame as the gentle-bred Colonel he was just as nosey in
getting his full share of the scratching.

With the stiff brush, Virginia would go to work on 'em, and the positions the colts would sometimes twist themselves into to get the most advantage of the scratching was comical. She would work on 'em until her arms about gave out, then spreading a healing and powerful salve of her own dad's mixing where the flies would be the most irritating, and which would be sure to keep them away until the next evening, the colts seeming all relieved would then go to grazing.

Brad, happening to catch her hard at work on the colts that way one evening, had to laugh some as he watched her from the corrals, then he started towards her. She seen him coming, packing a long grin on his face, she smiled back and being her arms was getting tired she could use him.

"Just in time, Brad," she says, handing him the brush. "My arms have given out. These spoiled ones seem to be getting biger and need more scratching every day."

"Which one have you been working on?" Brad asks, taking the brush.

"Both of 'em, at the same time as much as I can. If I work on only one the other would sure tramp me down."

Brad was in the pasture to help her most every evening after that. He was about sure she'd be there at that time too, as long as there'd be any flies to bother the colts, and them flies would be sure to last until late the next fall.

The two met in the pasture that way for quite a spell,

and with them meetings and conversation there'd be they got to be much looked forward to, by both.

It was during one of them that, while Brad was brushing Colonel's fine mane, Virginia watching him and the easy way he was doing it, remarked:

"He's getting very pretty, isn't he?"

"Sure is," Brad grinned. "Always was."

"That's true, and you shouldn't have given him to me."

"Eh, what?—" Brad turned to her, surprised. "But you like him and want him, don't you?"

"Why of course. But you would have so much more use for him than I ever would. While following your rodeos he'd make you a good fast horse for calf roping, and he might be fast enough so he could be used in the regular races, at least the relay races."

"Yeh"—says Brad, sort of thoughtful, but not about the possibilities of the colt. "Yeh, there's no doubt but what he'll be fast enough."

"Yes, just that," Virginia went on. "He'll be so fast he'd pass a long-legged wild steer and never even see him, let alone try to turn him."

Brad, looking at Colonel's long slim legs and trim ankles, had to admit to her that she was right. It was what he well knew, that he was all race horse.

"Sure," he finally says, "and I guess there won't be much use in trying to teach him anything about the tricky range cow, but something might come up where he might be handy. And that's for you to worry about," he laughed. "I'm no Indian giver. I gave you the horse, you accepted him, and you clinched the deal, not only with a handshake but with a kiss too, and that alone would make any man a criminal if he was to back out of the deal afterwards, or a criminal in getting more horses."

Virginia, seeing now that he wouldn't be wanting the colt back, felt relieved and pleased, and she didn't try to hide that when she smiled and spoke.

"I just wanted to make sure," she says. "Because I wouldn't want to have him taken away from me after I go to the work of training and making a winner of him."

And not to be outdone, Brad wrote out a long bill of sale of the colt to her that evening and tied it on the horn of her saddle where she'd be sure to find it the next morning.

But even with all of that the whole thing seemed to be just so much play for Virginia still felt the colt wasn't altogether hers, that Brad still had a hold on him. And Brad, having a hunch of that, somehow felt the same way.

There was only one thing to do, as both got to figuring by themselves, and that was to forget about the feeling and go according to the deal agreed on, with a good bill of sale for proof.

Neither spoke any more on the subject during the evenings that followed. They was careful not to.

Then one fine morning, after the other boys had rode into the ranch from their winter camps, more saddle horses was gathered, a wagon cleaned up and loaded with grub, the whole outfit started out for the range for the spring works, leaving Virginia to do what riding there was around the ranch.

But there was very little riding to be done close to the ranch now, the herd she'd been keeping tab on had been turned out, all excepting a few stragglers, and outside of keeping watch and seeing that no stock broke into the hay meadows, or that the rodeo stock didn't break out and such like, which all *had* to be attended to, there was hardly enough riding for her to keep her saddle warm. One of the ranch hands would bring in the milk cows and also seen that all the fences was kept up.

Somehow tho, she managed to "find" some riding when she wanted it, and besides what she needed to do. Like with any other work, there's always more can be done. Then with what all she could do in the house and around she never got lonesome, never while at the ranch. Fact is she was sort of glad when all the riders was gone, that gave her more responsibility, and especially with Brad's going she now felt as she went down to the pasture and colts of evenings that Colonel was sure enough all hers. She'd felt that way all the while he was gone during the winter, and couldn' understand why she didn't feel the same when he came back. Now he'd be away fairly steady for quite a spell, and on his return it'd be about time for him and Red and Jim to start out with the rodeo stock again. Then she'd have all summer, until away late in the fall to feel that Colonel was all hers some more.

That same feeling was also shared by Brad, while he was away, that the colt wasn't his no more then, but that he still had a hold on him when he'd return, and it was such a feeling that neither could buy or sell away, near like that of a kin.

Colonel was now over a year old, Virginia had learned that from the bill of sale which Brad had tied to her saddle, and to her he seemed to've got mighty tall for his age, and so narrow built. She sometimes had to laugh as him and little Charro, side by side, would come to meet her, for, poor little stunted Charro, even tho only a few months younger, looked near like a Shetland colt along-side of him.

But Charro was now fast losing his bloated-looking middle, rounding out in good shape in other places that should and looked as tho he'd some day be a good tough little horse, even if he might not turn out to win any show prize for looks. He'd never be as tall as Colonel but he'd be broader and of the breed that could sure cover the rough hills. His color, too, now that he was shed off slick wasn't so bad. It was kind of light blue roan turning to buckskin at the flanks and legs. He would be hard to see in the badland country where he'd been foaled.

A few weeks went by all peaceful, and one evening, as Virginia and Anne was on the lawn watering flowers and doing such like work, Cal and three others rode into the main corral. From the distance to them, Virginia recognized one as Brad, by the way he rode, and at that she somehow thought right away of Colonel. The sud-denness of the thought made her wonder at the time.

But she soon forgot, for during the next couple of

days them three riders got busy preparing to hit out, this time for rounds of the season's rodeos when they'd be gone until late fall again. The bucking horses was corralled and looked over well, a few of the old ones, also others that wasn't much more inclined to buck was cut out to be left behind, the old ones to be turned out to freedom and the young ones to be sold. These was replaced by fresh mean ones that was rearing to do their best that way, and all together, there couldn't be a tougher and more fit bunch of outlaws.

It went the same with the longhorn steers and bulls. There was no need of wasting motion to drop a hat for them to fight, and they was near out of shape with the lumps of fat they was packing, too fat to really do well in the arenas. But they'd lose some of that with the travelling and shipping and would then be in fine condition to do their best at their worst.

Two more riders came to take them out, and as it would take three days for the cattle to reach the shipping point they was started one day ahead. It would take only two for the horses to make the same distance, and early the following morning, Brad and Red and Jim started out with the buckers.

Cal and Virginia was at the corrals to wish 'em luck, and as the big gate swung open, Brad's parting remark to Virginia was, with a grin:

"And don't forget, too much sugar ain't good for him."

The girl smiled back at him like as much as to say that now he'd be gone, she'd feel Colonel would be all hers again and would do as she pleased with him. She understood that his remark was only in a joking way, along with the little dig that he still had something to say about the colt. For he knew that she'd never gave Colonel or any of her horses sugar.

With the going of Brad, Virginia had to laugh at herself some for the relief she felt in now having the colt all her own, also in realizing that Brad knew of her feelings that way.

That soon went out of her mind as she once again took "full possession" of Colonel and put him thru his paces, which was to do nothing but hunt his own shade, water and reach down for the clover and blue joint which made up the sod of the good-sized pasture. He also had to be good to Charro and not beat him in every race they'd have, nor crowd him away when Virginia came near to visit with 'em, rub and scratch their now smooth and shiny hides.

Summer came on with the regular routine of the ranch going well. Virginia, now having no more studying to do in preparing for winter's terms at college, had more time to be riding with her dad, and sometimes would be gone two and three days with him on big outside circle of the range, visiting neighboring cowfolks the while and bringing back what stock might have strayed.

The two also drove away a couple of times and took on early and small rodeos close by, of just a few days to each. Then come time for a bigger rodeo, a four day one, including the Fourth of July, and being that Cal's string of outlaw buckers and longhorns had been contracted for that particular contest, there was nothing but what him and Virginia should jump in the car and roll on over to attend. It was a good long day's drive to the town where the rodeo would be held, and with the four days of it and all, Cal figured they'd be gone about a week.

It was a good time for him to go too, Cal thought, for there would be no rushing work needing his attention at the ranch right along then, besides he'd be leaving one good man to take charge of the ranch work and two cowboys to take care of the riding in general. He could take his time, enjoy watching his outlaw stock perform and come back when he durned pleased.

As for Virginia, she would still had less to worry about on her trip. There was of course the colts and her three good saddle horses which she prized near as much as her dad did the whole ranch and stock, and she couldn't see where, in the good and well fenced pasture they was in, any harm could come to 'em in any way, shape or form. Not any more than if she stayed on the spot and stood guard over 'em.

So, all free of cares, the two was all for the pleasure that was ahead. Cal to see his stock come out of the chutes and doing their worst, and Virginia with about the same enthusiasm, also sort of laughing at the thought of returning Brad's joking remark by having him see that she'd "deserted" Colonel for the time, and telling him he wouldn't be getting his sugar while she was away.

The rodeo opened with a bang and stayed wild during

Summer came on with the regular routine of the ranch going well

every performance of the four days. Cal was more than pleased the way his stock tore things up, and when all was over, the dust settled and Brad came out with the honors of first prize in bronc riding on Cal's own worst buckers that put the cap on the best of his expectations.

As for Virginia, for punishment in deserting the colt she was taken into custody by Brad and she wasn't to go to dances, other entertainment nor eating places with any one else but him or Cal, or Red or Jim, or maybe a few of the other cowboys he knew, if she'd be good. She had to be good.

They was two tired but very pleased people when Cal and Virginia drove into the ranch late during the night of the day after the rodeo was over, and the girl didn't at all hear the early chirping of the birds when the next morning come. Cal didn't do much better, and as the two gathered for the late breakfast Anne had fixed for 'em they sort of went over the few fast days of the rodeo with her, telling her of what a great contest it had been, Brad winning first prize in bronc riding, Red first in bull-dogging and Jim second in steer riding and roping, and so on.

Anne was pleased to know and listened well, but seemed to be staying away in the kitchen more than she had before, especially after they'd return from a trip, when she'd be anxious to hear all they'd have to say. Her smile wasn't all there either when she'd be told of some funny things that happened during the rodeo, and Virginia, finally noticing her strange lack of interest, got to wondering. She wondered some more as Anne sort of dodged her every look but she only kept quiet at that, finished her breakfast and waited until her dad was thru and went outside.

"What is it, Anne?" Virginia asked soon as Cal was out of hearing, "Something wrong?"

"Well, not exactly," says Anne, who now seemed anxious to speak. "It's just that Colonel and the other little colt with him got out of the pasture and got away. Mr. Jack (the cowboy who'd done the riding at the ranch) says they got away a couple of days before he missed 'em, then he seen where two gates had been left open, like a purpose."

Virginia tried to keep calm. "When was it they got away, do you know, Anne—and who could have left the gates open?

"Mr. Jack says he figured it was about a day after you left, as far as he could tell—This young town feller your dad hired some time back, the one who wanted to learn to be a cowboy, is the one who left the gates open." Anne was quick to get to the boy's rescue there. "But he realized what a bad mistake he'd made," she went on "and he right away told Mr. Jack about it. But it was too late then, the colts had a couple of days head start."

Virginia tried to cheer herself with the hope that they couldn't have gone far, maybe no farther than the first bunch of horses on the horse range and would just wander around there.

But Anne sort of shattered that hope when she went on to say that Jack had rode the whole horse range without seeing any sign of 'em. "He didn't want to stay away from the ranch," she said, "but he did and stayed two days and one night, rode well into the wild horse country and still couldn't see any sign of 'em. So he decided to wait till you folks come back and then ride that country well.

"From what Jack says," Anne went on, "them colts are sure enough in the wild horse country, with some wild bunch. But I wouldn't worry too much about 'em, Virginia. They'll——"

Virginia didn't wait to hear any more. She dashed away to her bed room and went to reaching for her riding clothes."

A MUSTANGER'S RIG

WILL JAMES

CHAPTER SIX

BADLANDS AND LIONS

AS much as it had been a puzzle and confusing to Colonel when he'd been loaded in the horse trailer and whizzed away from his home pastures some eight months past, the long scary ride on the train amongst the strange horses afterwards, then the winter at the ranch and all, this which he was now experiencing was near as much of a puzzle and confusing. This being away out, in a wild country and nothing to stop him from roaming on and on.

Little Charro had been the first one to notice the pasture gate being opened. This only left 'em into a big field where stock was kept off and hay would later be cut and stacked for the winter's feeding. But with the colts' natural curiosity, and as they went to exploring and rambling over the big field, Charro found another gate and there he took the lead once more, thru the last opening to the big outside and freedom.

That was the last fence, and the little wild colt, feeling the openness in his blood, the sense any wild creature keeps even tho maybe raised in captivity, stuck his nose in the air, smelled of the earth and looked all around, near like a freedom-loving human released from

110

prison, and even more appreciating, for there was more freedom bred in one drop of his blood than there could be in all of any human being.

The air and warm breezes had been the same in the good green pasture and field he'd just left, but now, out of them, it was like, well, like freedom, and that's all needs to be said, for that can't be described.

Little Charro took the lead in a slow walk, sniffing at near every bush he passed and once in a while stop to look all around him. He zigzagged considerable as he went, followed none of the plain trails that was along the fence bordering the ranch and went acrost many after leaving it, but with all his aimless-like travelling he was heading straight for one direction, that of his home range and where his wild horse instinct drawed him.

With Colonel there was an entirely different feeling. To him, there really was no home, no range. With his past experiences and like jerked away from where his instinct dwelled, that all had become a blur. The only home he knew now was that of the ranch, and he was going away from there into another strange world, creating in him another strange feeling.

This was one time when, with all his speed, he didn't race ahead of his little pardner, Charro. For in him he not only felt confidence but that he was leading him into a great adventure, and much like one youngster following another braver one thru dark woods to haunted houses and caves, he was curious but glad to only follow.

Every once in a while, when Charro would stop to take a look all around and sniff at the air, Colonel would also do the same, but most always in only one direction, and that was back the way he come, the ranch. It wasn't so much that he wanted to return there as the feeling that he was leaving all touch with humans, the care his breed was so used to, and heading out for the unknown. He sometimes listened as tho Virginia was calling him and would get to wondering if he should go on. But Charro, not at all wondering that way, kept on a going, and half for fear of being left behind, alone, and again curious as to what might lay ahead he'd catch up with him.

This was something like the time when he was trailed in from the railroad to the ranch. There was the company of humans then, and even tho he couldn't realize very much at the time and he was now much stronger and bigger, the sun was shining instead of a blizzard howling, he had the same feeling of strange adventure, sort of confusing and scary with so much openness, and being able to go where he pleased, nothing to stop him was mighty new to him. He'd felt easier if Virginia or Brad had been along.

Or maybe he should of stayed by the saddle horses him and Charro had been pasturing with. Them had been wise and stayed where the good grass was, but Charro and him had gone on, on to where now they was well out in the open and in rough country, on the horse range, and the tall trees of the ranch couldn't be seen no more.

The bunch was in a steep hollow, a water hole was in the bottom

Bunches of horses was now and again sighted when the horse range was reached, and Colonel was for going towards every bunch that was seen, for no reason only maybe to satisfy his curiosity and getting acquainted, but little Charro wouldn't have none of that, and instead of going near, made a good circle around and past 'em.

But, near of a sudden, they come onto a bunch that Charro hadn't seen and couldn't get to dodge. The bunch was in a steep hollow, a water hole was in the bottom and the horses was watering there. The colts no more than seen the bunch below when Colonel soon learned the reason why his little pardner had dodged such bunches. For at one glance of the colts a wicked looking, long-maned black stallion left the bunch and came on a high lope to meet 'em. Little Charro, sensing danger, lit out as fast as he could for a wild plum thicket and hid, while Colonel, seeing no more harm in the black than there'd been with the outlaw buckers he'd got to know as being friendly, kind of wondered at Charro's actions.

But he didn't get to wonder long. For the black stallion, much against having a strange one even looking at his bunch, charged into Colonel with all his teeth, hoofs and weight, without warning, folded him up like an accordion and sent him a sailing to roll quite a few times before he come to a dazed footing.

He was still in a daze when the stallion lit into him again, but this time Colonel also got to sensing what little Charro already knew, and instead of holding his ground like in friendly meeting he started to moving, moving as fast as he could and away from that murderous black. But being sort of knocked out of wind he didn't get away fast enough, and this time the stallion champed his teeth on the back of his neck. The fact that Colonel was now trying to slip away was all that saved him from a broken neck.

As it was, he was sent a rolling once more. But not as hard as before, and when he got up it was fairly clear in his mind that he should get to running as quick and as fast as he could. That he did, but the stallion would of got him again, only, maybe it was only by chance but little Charro showed himself about then and attracted the stallion's attention, and that saved Colonel's neck.

The black stopped just long enough to investigate little Charro, which by then had again got in the thick of the thorny plum thicket and where the openings was too low for the big horse to follow, besides, Charro was still too much of a colt for the stallion to get after. By the time the black got thru his investigation, Colonel was well away at a safe distance and still a going. The stallion looked his direction, shook his head in defiance and warning and went back to his bunch down by the water hole.

Colonel's size had been his downfall there. He was only a few months past yearling but near as tall if not near as broad as the stallion, where, with little Charro, still a few months short of being a yearling, and with his stunted growth he looked more like a six-month-old colt.

But the wild instinct of his past generations wasn't stunted any, neither was his brain, and now with the good care of the past winter he could well follow on the trail of his ancestors again.

With the surprise and scare that Colonel had got he'd kept on running until he begin to tire. When he finally slowed down and then stopped he was quite some distance from where he'd met the stallion and left Charro, and looking around some he seen he was well on his way back to the ranch. He looked around some more, for Charro now, and not seeing him anywhere he was sort of up a stump as to what to do. He missed his little pardner very much right then, for he was still mighty scared. He nickered for him but of course there was no answer.

He stood for a spell, just looking around, then he realized he was thirsty. The run had sweated him up considerable, then there was a big gash on the top of his neck where some of his hide and flesh was missing. Blood was running pretty free from that, making him still thirstier and some weaker.

The last water he'd seen was where the stallion and his bunch had been, but he was far from hankering to go back to that place as yet, and now that he was alone and so well on his way back to the ranch he was kind of debating as to which way to-turn. It would be kind of hard to go by his lonesome now, being he was so attached to little Charro. But could he find Charro again? He knew he could find the ranch, and water on the way there.

He sort of circled around a few steps at a time then, like hardly realizing or caring which way he went, he headed back the direction of the water hole and where he'd last seen Charro.

And Charro, also far from wanting to lose his long legged pardner, had got out of his hiding place after the stud bunch had watered and gone, went to take a drink himself and then, instead of hitting for his home range which had been his intention he went back the way Colonel had gone, towards the ranch. But he wasn't travelling very fast, not near as fast as Colonel had in getting away from the stallion. He just trotted and walked along, sniffing of the brush as wild horses do for the scent and kept looking ahead for sight of him.

Colonel wasn't very fast on his return to the water hole either, and sometimes he'd stop to look back the direction of the ranch, wondering if to go on. But always the thought of little Charro would win him over and he'd poke along towards where he'd last been with him.

He was poking along that way, not at all thinking that Charro would also be on the hunt for him, when coming to the sharp point of a brush covered ledge and seeing a horse in the shadow heading his way, Colonel lost all thoughts of Charro, snorted his féar that it might be the stallion and, without taking a second look, scampered out into more open country. He'd went on some more, only he heard a loud nicker, and turning in his tracks he then recognized Charro coming out of the brush. It was with great surprise and pleasure as he nickered back and trotted on to meet him—. It would

be a long time before Colonel would come up in friendly
greeting to a strange range horse, but he still had some
more to learn about that, that all wasn't such as the
black stallion.

Now that the two got together again there was a little
horse talk as to what next and which way. Colonel, now
satisfied and feeling safer with his little pardner being
near, thought only of water and took the lead this time,
for the water hole, and too thirsty right then to think
of what had happened to him there not so long before.

Not a horse was in sight as the two neared the water
hole, nor none by it as Colonel now took care of first
peeking down into it. He then went down while Charro
sort of kept watch up above. Colonel quenched his thirst
some, and now he done one thing which he'd never done
before and which surprised him as much as how good
it felt, he got down to his knees at the edge of the
muddy water hole, then on his side and went on rolling
in the few inches of water and sticky mud. The flies is
what had decided him to do that, they'd been pestering
him considerable, especially the raw gash on his neck
and where the blood streamed down along it. The water
and sticky mud felt good, and he wallowed in it with the
same enjoyment as a mud hen would and done about as
good a job plastering himself.

When he stood up he was all of a buckskin color with
mud, not at all like the thoroughbred he was and the
son of the great Montezuma. But that sure didn't worry
him any right then, the mud plastering would keep the
flies away, and now the raw and bleeding gash was also

well covered and protected. It would still be when the mud dried and caked, so would most of his body.

He went further into the pool, took a few more swallows of clearer water and, now much refreshed went up out of the hole to join little Charro, ready to travel on some more.

Charro took the lead from there on, and now, from his experience with the stallion, Colonel had of a sudden realized that it would be well for him to follow that little feller's lead mighty close and not go ahead of him if he wanted to stay all together, to dodge when he did and do all as he did in the future.

They travelled along, grazing as they went, and it was good when night come and they got up high on a little strip of bench land where the strong grass was aplenty and a cool breeze fanned their hides. They rested there, their first night away from the ranch, and wether it was from being some tired or getting a faint realization of the great feeling of freedom, Colonel was very satisfied, even after that day's experience and stinging of his hurts, for that all went with the spirit of adventure, a sort of spice which made freedom sort of exciting, where there's no law and the main protection is wisdom, alertness, speed and strength.

There may be sudden death, or sometimes long lean spells during droughts and hard winters, but that can also happen to the domestic and stabled animal, and besides them being burdened with hard work or training there's none of the great freedom, doing as pleases, or rolling in the mud and such like which goes with freedom.

They stayed on the high bench all that night. When the sun came up they looked around as they sunned themselves and listened at the faint noises of the wild which they could hear for a long ways in the stillness of the morning. They could also see for many miles all around 'em, and finally stretching themselves from their standing position they started on the move again, Charro taking the lead down over the edge of the high land and headed for the most broken up, unnatural and spooky looking country Colonel had ever seen. It looked as tho the devil himself had done the carving of that land, and the coloring, running in strips from sun-bright to night-dark, varied so it was mighty all colorful, but also like as if the devil still kept the fires burning there.

To look at the land from the high bench where the colts had been, a stranger would think it waterless, grassless and that not a breathing thing could live in it. It would seem as some mighty pretty and just as awful a country, a wild stretch to just look at and pass on by from a good distance. But getting down into the depth of that country, as the colts was now doing, the stranger would of been surprised and seen big tufts of strong grass amongst the crags and in scattering patches of scrub brush of all kinds. There was also water, little springs bubbling up out of the earth or seeping thru lava-rock ledges. Them springs was far apart and some very poisonous, as the bleached bones of animals around 'em would show.

There was also game in that country, such as rabbit and deer, and that made it good country for mountain lion and cayote, especially the lion, for, along with that game was also wild horses, and there's no meat the lion likes better than that of a yearling colt. It was the wild horse country, the lion's lair and taking the place of the devil himself, and there's where, in the heart of that country, Charro and Colonel was trailing.

The lion had picked that country for the same reason the wild horse had. It was their last refuge from the crowding of the human, and they'd been throwed together that way the same as floods makes all races scramble for high points.

After getting down over the rim of the high bench and into that unpromising looking land, Colonel sort of felt that a big gate had closed after him and would keep him from ever coming back, that he would become a different kind of a horse and real adventure would now begin. The strangeness of the country of course had a lot to do with making him feel that way, but as he wound around steep, needle-like pinnacles in following Charro, where it sometimes looked as tho the bottom was a mile down, and no place for solid footing while skirting the steep places, he felt that the adventuring was sure enough beginning.

There was places where he more than hesitated, and stopped, hardly thinking he could make it, and it was at such times, as he watched Charro going on unconcerned-like, that he wished he had such short legs as he had or could handle his own long ones as well.

When he'd come to such places he'd look up or down for some way of getting around, but there seldom was, and one time when he did try getting around such a dangerous place he of a sudden found himself bogged down to his belly in dry looking earth. It was dry but full of air pockets and powdery, and when he struggled to get out of there he went a rolling down the side of the pinnacle, all the way down to the bottom, and a few more such powdery places along the way was all that checked him from a mighty hard landing at the bottom——.

There was another instance that reminded him of how he should follow little Charro, if he could, and do as he did.

Where Charro got all his knowledge was of course not from his mother's teachings for he hadn't been with her long enough, but it was from her blood and breeding. He'd inherited her instinct which was that of the wild horse, like with any other wild animal, and even tho he still had plenty to learn, this which he did know or felt would stand him in mighty good stead, and give him a big advantage over the tall turf-bred colt which followed his lead.

Colonel of course had his own inheritance in instinct but not of the kind that fitted where he was, no more than Charro's would with the turf and such doings.

But it sure wasn't Colonel's fault to be where he was, and when he'd come to scary places and doings he'd also liked mighty well to've been on good level earth and amongst all he was bred for. He hadn't cared to leave his home away to the east but that couldn't be helped, and later when he'd got used to the ranch and left it, it wasn't because he really wanted to but because he didn't know any better, then the sense of freedom gave him a strange feeling and he'd wanted to know more about it, naturally. But little Charro was the guilty one there, for, without him taking the lead, Colonel would have stayed with the saddle horses at the ranch.

But it was too late now, for, Colonel had sort of burned his bridges behind him (as the saying goes), he wouldn't of tried to come back on the same trail Charro had taken him, and he sure wouldn't try any other for fear it might be still worse. He wouldn't leave Charro anyhow, not now no more.

So, as it was, Colonel would have to make the best of his "freedom," even if he'd sometimes come to wish he was in some safe corral or paddock and humans was near.

That strange and exciting feeling of freedom and adventure got to sort of wearing out on him as the days went by, especially after another "very exciting" experience one fine day—. Him and Charro was grazing on a steep and lava terraced side of a hill when, for no reason that Colonel could see, Charro of a sudden raised his head, looked above to a ledge, snorted, and at once scrambled down the steep hill like the very devil was after him, and Colonel, now having well learned that such quick action from Charro meant that he should do the same and as quick, tumbled down the hill right after him, and not any too soon, for right behind him was a tawny streak of lion which, seeming like to drop out of thin air, was close to within claw reach of his tail.

Right behind him was a tawny streak of lion which, seeming like to drop
out of thin air, was close to within claw reach of his tail

A lion can make very good speed for a short distance, specially coming down a hill, but Colonel getting one very fleeting glance at that one, and not even knowing what it was nor how dangerous it might be, also made very good speed, and to his own surprise as well as Charro's, made the bottom on all fours and still a running.

The lion had eased around and perched himself above the colts, as he'd seen 'em graze, waited until they might graze closer so he could spring on 'em, and it was only the sense of being watched, like it sometimes happens even with humans, that made Charro look up, and getting only a glimpse of the tawny hair shining to the sun had been enough for him, and the lion, knowing he'd been seen, lost no time and sprung. But the distance had been too great.

Reaching the bottom and in a level dry wash, the colts easy left the lion a safe distance behind, and now, Colonel, all spooked up, right away passed Charro on the level stretch. In his stampeding that way he run on without realizing he left Charro behind also, and then, like out of nowhere there come another lion, right in front of him and blocking the narrow wash where, at that point, the walls was straight up.

Some away back and asleep instinct must of come to life sudden in Colonel's think tank right then, for, at the sight of the lion, he stopped as if he'd run into a stone wall, and he didn't stand to palaver nor try to go past him either. A good cowhorse couldn't of turned and picked up speed any faster than Colonel did, and then realizing that Charro wasn't near he more than tore the earth on his way back up the wash.

The second lion being also taken by surprise at the sudden sight of Colonel, and not prepared for attack, couldn't and didn't even try to follow that long legged streak of horseflesh. He just snarled his disappointment, sat on his haunches and glared at him as he disappeared around a turn in the wash.

Colonel was still coming full speed, head high and looking behind to see if the lion was coming when, making the turn, he near bumped into Charro, and then he stopped short again.

Little Charro hadn't been running much, not after he seen that first lion had stopped following, and now he was just busy sort of stalking that animal which had stirred such a fear in him, wondering why, when Colonel come a busting in on him and interrupted his investigation with another scare.

Now they was between two full grown and mighty hungry acting lions, and the deep wash they was into, with the high and steep walls on both sides, had 'em in about the same fix as "Daniel in the lion's den," only with no Divine Power to protect 'em.

But little Charro didn't seem to be much scared and that sort of calmed Colonel some. For one thing, Charro had found out that he could outrun the yellowish, taillashing, silent-moving creature, and even tho he sensed it was mighty dangerous to get near he had a fair idea of how close he could get and still be safe. He knew that the animal was mighty quick, but so was he, and now that he had him spotted he was for getting closer and watch it for a spell, not knowing that he couldn't get away very far now in case he had to, for only a few hundred yards down the wash was the other lion which would sure nab him or Colonel if they tried to get past. Then again that second lion might close up on 'em, and, well, then the colts would soon be just lion meat.

Charro, with Colonel close behind, went on with his investigating the first lion, and that wise one, full of many tricks, went to work on Charro's curiosity. He went his silent way to the thick brush where the colts had been grazing, and showing just enough of himself there so the colt would come closer for a better look, he waited. When the nosey colt did come closer the lion then went on thru the patch of brush, to circle up to the ledge where he'd sprung off of once before. He now had the colt close enough to it so he'd sure get him this time.

But getting near that ledge again and seeing the lion disappear thru the brush sort of left Charro nervous, with a strong hunch that he'd better move. There was nothing to stop him from doing that and he did move, just in time again and with the same result as before, and now that his fun and investigating was over he was ready to go on again, down the wash, and then he spotted the other lion.

Well, now, Charro realized, as well as any human could, that this was serious. He stopped still in his tracks at the sight of the second lion, Colonel right by his side, like as much as to ask "Now what'll we do?"

But Charro wasn't stumped nor excited nor scared. That wasn't in his breed, not when it was time for straight thinking and fast action. He sized up both sides of the wash for a way out and at the steepness of 'em he seen where he'd made a big mistake, the mistake of getting into such a pocket and natural trap. The lion knew it and often made use of it that way.

The wash cut into the earth by centuries of rushing waters from cloudbursts and melting snows was walled on each side by from twenty to forty foot banks, straight up, and as Charro now went to looking around for an opening he seen only one which he figured him and Colonel *might* be able to make. This one chance wasn't exactly an opening but a steep slide of shale rock which had come down into the wash and near blocked it. It would be a mighty steep climb and where a horse might make one step and lose two in the loose shale.

But there was no other way out, Charro was sure of that. None excepting to make a rush past the lions, and a glance at them now restless meat eaters more than warned 'em against trying anything like that, unless— What's more they was, one from each side, beginning to close in on 'em, kind of slow but sort of measuring their distance and like they might make a rush most any time. Charro more than sensed that danger, and right at once, he decided to try and beat 'em to it and get out of there. Running his nose along Colonel's neck, which went as a signal for "Let's go," he made a running start for the steep shale slide, Colonel right after him, and at the same time, the lions seeing their intended victims trying to get away both made a rush for 'em.

It was quite some scramble from the start. There couldn't be no speed made, and it was a great wonder that any headway could be made at all, but there was a lot of fast pawing and reaching for footholts, and there, the colts, being in the lead and side by side, had the advantage, for in their scrambling to get up the slide they'd steady start another which the lions had to buck up against, along with the loose sharp rock that the colts' hoofs sent a-flying their way. They couldn't get no footing either in the sliding shale and was at times near buried in it. Their lunging didn't get 'em no closer to the colts, and with the pelting of the flying sharp shale they couldn't dodge and which more than hindered their seeing they finally had to let up and to figure on some other way of getting their prey.

As the lions watched the colts struggling up, slow but steady, and making it impossible for them to follow they knew there was no way of getting at 'em, not unless they went up or down the wash, got out and above the colts before they could get off the slide above the wash and on solid footing. Once the colts got there the lions wouldn't have no chance, and now they wouldn't have the time to get around and above before the colts did.

But there was still hope and another chance, for the lions. The colts, struggling, sliding and fighting their way up, was near to where they could get off the slide to the edge of the wash and on more solid footing, when, stopping for a much needed breathing spell, Charro once again raised his head in surprise and snorted his fear. For to the side of the slide and where he figured on getting off of it to solid ground he seen, a shining to the sun behind some low brush, the tops of rounded heads and flattened ears of two more lions.

He didn't make no wild dash away from there this time, and now it looked like him and Colonel was sure enough done for. Lions on top of the slide and lions at the bottom. Colonel, on account of Charro being between, didn't get to see the lions at the top and only wondering what Charro was snorting at kept ready to keep up with every move he made. Charro was again doing some tall figuring, sizing up the steep lay of the land and the positions of the meat eaters, and was about stumped as to what to do, when the lions at the bottom made him decide to do something, and mighty quick.

For now that the colts was standing still and there was no more sliding shale to hinder 'em they lunged and went to springing for them, and that started things, with the colts stirring a heap more shale to sliding and flying and that soon sent 'em back to the bottom. It was a great wonder the colts didn't also go back down in their desperate try and taking the one chance, which was sure a desperate one, for Charro had decided to try the other side of the slide, the opposite from where the lions above was, and it was a mighty dangerous place, for once there, and one misstep meant a thirty foot straight fall to the bottom of the wash, and the lions there.

But there was no choice now, and as scary as the spot

to safety would be to cross it wasn't as scary as the lions at the bottom and top. In his mightiest lunging and scrambling, Charro finally made it to the steep edge and sort of balanced there for a few seconds before going on and making room for Colonel, who also was doing some tall scrambling close to him and now had more fear of the lions than he did of the scary place. He didn't hesitate, and that was all that saved him.

But the odds was sure against him and, for a time, it looked like he was a gone goslin and would sure fall over backwards and down from the steep place. But he got to his knees, stretched his long neck, and seeming like to even use his chin to grab some hold he finally made it up to the side of Charro, his heart beating fit to bust.

There the two stood for a spell, now feeling at last safe from the lions and went to taking long breaths of much needed wind—. They'd made it.

CHAPTER SEVEN

CHARRO'S HOME RANGE

ONCE on top, above the shale slide, and well out of danger of being trapped or cornered, the colts both took a long breath of relief at the narrow escape and scare they'd had. They soon got to feeling pretty brave again in being free and in the open, also as curious as ever, and now that they was on safe ground, Charro wanted to investigate the two lions that'd been by the slide, for he sort of wondered why them two hadn't sprung at 'em from there. They'd had a good chance, all downhill and sliding, where the ones below didn't have any chance at all.

Circling above and past the slide, Charro soon spotted the two lions, still in the same place, and now taking a good look around to make sure for a good quick get away in case him and Colonel had to, Charro took the lead on down towards the lions. There seemed to be nothing ferocious about these much as he came closer, ready to turn and go to running any second. These was much smaller than the other two, and only seemed to want to hide. But Charro wasn't going to be fooled as he came still closer, and finally, getting still braver and too close for comfort, for the lions they showed their teeth at him, but got up and moved away. At that,

Charro got the feeling that these was scared of him, that he had 'em buffaloed. Then to carry on a big bluff he put his ears back, showed his own teeth and rushed at 'em. To his surprise and pleasure the bluff worked, Colonel then joined in on the fun and in mighty quick time had the two a-scampering and rushing for the slide where they rolled over and over and slid on down to meet the two big ones below, their papa and mamma. These two smaller ones was their youngsters, a whole family which the colts had bumped into.

That turn of events seemed to please the colts very much, like giving the big ones a real and good "horse laugh" in return for the scare they'd been given. Now satisfied, and leaving the big ones lashing their tails in disappointment, the colts went on to higher and more open grounds. They would go on following the high ridges from now on, until they was at least well out of that lion family's range.

But in that land they might get out of one such range only to get into another, and it would be well for them to keep on the alert always, keep away from overhanging ledges, watchful when going thru patches of jack pine or juniper, also keep out of other such boxed-in washes or canyons as they'd narrowly escaped out of, or any other place where a lion could hide and wait to spring from.

Well beaten trails to watering places are the most dangerous, and all such would be found out thru instinct to later be dodged more thru experience, and there would come a time when any such dangerous places would seem as well noticed as if a big sign was posted there, like with many other things the wild horse or game had to watch out for in that country, even to the human which, to them, was the most dangerous of all.

Quite a strip of such a country was covered during the few days that followed and nothing scary happened along the way much, only that they come acrost a rattlesnake now and again, but that didn't bother them, for the reptiles most of the time gave some warning that was well enough understood, and being they seemed anything but worth investigating they was just given plenty of room. Lizards of all kinds wasn't even noticed.

Cayotes was once in a while sighted and sometimes passed by to within a few yards, but they wasn't hardly paid any attention to either. Colonel thought they was only dogs. But if the colts would ever got bogged down or helpless in any way them harmless looking cayotes would turn to be as dangerous as any lion.

There'd been more lions too a watching the colts as they trailed along or grazed, but the colts didn't see any of them, for being they had now got some experience with them, and experience they profited by and wouldn't forget as long as they lived, they knew of the kind of country they'd hang out in and circled well around all such. The lions seen them only at safe distances and places.

Deer, also wise to the lion, was often seen in such places too, and the colts, only thru mild curiosity, would sometimes stop to graze among 'em, neither kind with any fear of one another. It was the same with the few

Quite a strip of such a country was covered during
the few days that followed

antelope that was in that country. The antelope belonged to the flat and open ranges, but like the wild
horse, and since the human hunted and crowded 'em out
of their rightful land, they also had to make the best
of the badlands and took refuge there.

The badlands would always be such a refuge, for no
matter how crowded the country around got the plow
could never level or tame that barren land to farming.
Even the hunters would seldom get in there, for it was
a near impossible country to ride in a-horseback, and

being there was well timbered mountains with good trout streams in other parts, the badland strip was left pretty well alone by them. A prospector would wander in once in a while, but it was soon found that the colors there was all color and not of gold.

There was also the lion hunter who'd come to get at the big "cats" for the bounty that was hung up for their scalp, and them was the real friends to the game and horses there as well as in other ranges around, but he was dodged too, for, going by all other humans he was only a killer and not to be trusted.

The wild horse runner was another to be dodged, as much as the deer had to dodge the hunter. The wild horse runner would set traps of wire and cedar corrals in them badlands and so well built and fitting to the country that a wild horse would often find himself closed into one without hardly knowing. These traps would be around water holes, and the gate would be sprung closed while the horses would be inside of it, drinking.

All in all the badlands was well named when considering what all every living thing in it had to keep watching out for. Even the snake and lizard wasn't safe, and neither was the spider, centipede and scorpion which they lived on, for, in turn, the eagle, buzzard and hawk would get them too.

With their rambling in such country, the colts made out well enough, even if sometimes it was a long time between drinks. For a few days after the skirmish with the lions, Charro led on pretty well one direction, and even tho in having to wind around considerable, like covering eight miles of twisting ridges to make one straight one, getting around unpassable deep cuts, towering cliffs and such, and in their travelling, taking their time, and seeming aimless was, after all, pretty straight towards one point, where the sun would be setting of evenings, and a good many miles was covered in that direction. Maybe only fifty miles as the bird flies but more like a hundred and fifty as any hoofed animal would have to go to've followed their trail.

And their winding trail would be hard to follow, for it being most always on high ridges, sometimes so narrow that only one could go along at a time, and where the wind blowed most always, a hoof print would soon be blurred away or show no sign on the hard earth and rock.

Only a couple of small bunches of wild horses was seen during the first few days of the colts' rambling, for they ranged in that dry and hot country mostly during winters only, for need of shelter, and they could do a long time without water there when the snows come and banked up in the many crags.

Charro didn't let up much on his lead thru that country and it was quite a few days from the time him and Colonel left the ranch when he at last didn't seem to want to go any further, only to graze and water in one scope of country at the edge of the badlands. It was where his mother had ranged and where he'd been foaled, his home range, and he'd come to it as natural as any grown horse would. (It's been known of wild horses travelling four and five hundred miles so as to get back to their home range, going thru towns and settlements, crossing bridges and many such places where they couldn't be driven thru by rider.)

Once again on his home range, Charro seemed satisfied not to go beyond it, and even tho he'd been only about a month old when his mother and him and the bunch they was with had been chased from it by wild horse runners, was many miles away from there when he couldn't go no further and was left behind he still knew his home range, the water holes and the boundaries of it.

His mother and the bunch had most likely been caught, and as for himself, having been left far away from his home range, then in looking for his mother and rambling on some more, like lost, suffering and not realizing where he was going when Brad found him there was no telling how far he'd strayed. But with his return to life and strength while at the ranch his wild instinct also returned, and as gentle and tame as he'd been there it wasn't his true nature and the call of his home range got stronger right along as he'd come back to life. Then the pasture and field gates had been found open.

Charro didn't go to looking for his mother when he got back to his home range. Fact is he wouldn't of known her if he'd seen her, for, like Colonel, he was well weaned so's to entirely forget all about her, him by his suffering and then the long winter at the ranch, and Colonel by the long and strange distance and the change of climate.

Where Charro still had some advantage over Colonel was that he still had a range that was natural home to him, where Colonel had none. But that didn't seem to matter much to the thoroughbred no more, for all was so strange and interesting, and even tho he did think of the home pastures and missed the company of humans once in a while he was now fast beginning to get weaned away from that too. His home would now be on Charro's home range.

At the edge of the badlands where it was there was more shade, water and grass, also when in danger of mustang runners there was always the thick of the badlands to hit for and make a getaway into. For that reason there was more horses along there. Not a day or night passed but two or three bunches was seen, and at the sight of each bunch, Colonel was no more for running towards and meeting 'em. He'd learned one good lesson as to that, the one when the black stallion had near took him apart, and that was another experience he'd never forget for as long as he lived. He still very much felt the scar of that meeting.

Charro, being already wise and mighty careful that way, wasn't for making acquaintance with any bunch right quick, nor even show himself to 'em. A right bunch would come along sometime at the right time and then would be time enough. He was plenty satisfied to be just with Colonel, and even tho that long legged pal of his needed plenty of watching and coaching that only gave him a feeling of responsibility which he had plenty of time for and enjoyed, like being "big brother" or

leader, and Colonel more than looked up to him that
way, even if Charro was near a foot shorter and some
months younger.

But, as things went so well with the two runaways,
the feeling sure didn't carry over the badlands to the
Hip O ranch, where now, Virginia was doing a heap
of fretting, riding and squinting in trying to track 'em
down.

She of course knew right away on her return from
her trip that they'd got out of the pasture and then
the big field, she'd seen their tracks on the outside there
but being them tracks was about a week old by then,
was so blown and tracked over there was no following
them to any distance, not even as far as the horse range.
All she got out of the tracks was the general direction
the colts had taken, but she couldn't very well go by
that either because what little she got by the tracks was
so winding and aimless-like that there was hardly no
telling where they might of went after they got to the
horse range, where the tracks had led to and vanished.

Another thing was, that what little she could get from
the tracks as to where they'd be headed, was another
direction from where Brad had found little Charro, and
where she figured was his home range and would go back
to. She knew wild horses and their ways well but she
didn't know that the colt had been so far away from his
home range at the time when he'd been found.

She knew, too, that that "little rascal," as she now
and again called Charro, had been the leader in the

get-away, that Colonel would never have gone on by
himself, took the lead or left the saddle horses which
hadn't tried to go.

But knowing that didn't help her any. She at first
rode the horse range well, thinking and hoping that
they would be with or near some bunch there. She accounted for and looked thru every bunch, even the stud
bunches which she knew they wouldn't be with, but she
let no chance pass by, and finally making sure they
wasn't on the horse range she went to skirting the badlands, sometimes partways into them and wouldn't get
back to the ranch until after dark, on a very tired horse.

But, on another and fresh horse, she'd be out again
early the next morning, made big circles at different
points from the ranch, inquire from neighbor cowfolks
which was a day's ride away and where she'd sometimes
stay for the night.

There wasn't a bunch of horses to within forty miles
in every direction of the ranch that she didn't look thru,
and with the neighbors also being on the look out that
made quite a stretch of country that would be covered.
Over a hundred miles from the ranch, in some parts.

Of all the country being covered and riders being
on the lookout there was only *one* that Virginia didn't
think of, and that was the very same one the colts now
was in, beyond the badland strip. There was good and
plain enough reasons why she never thought of that
being the country they would be in. One was that she
figured that was away off from where she figured
Charro's home range to be, from where Brad had found

All the country being covered and riders being on the lookout

him, and that led her off, with another good reason that
the colts would never try to cross them badlands.

Then one day, after she'd covered every part of the

range she could think of where the colts might be in, she asked her dad if he would have Brad ride the country where he'd found Charro. She'd already rode close to it herself but not as much as she'd wanted to, for it being mighty barren and a long ways she couldn't make it and be back to the ranch for that night.

Brad having got back to the ranch for a short spell between rodeos would be glad to go, for as her dad told her, he'd been near as worried about the colts, especially Colonel, as she was and he was anxious to get 'em back.

"And I'll do better than that," Cal had went on to tell her. "I'll send Red with him, and a pack horse with grub and bedding so they can make camp and ride from there for a few days, if necessary. But I'll do that only on one condition, Virginia," he'd added on, "and that's that you stay home and rest up for a spell. You're about all in and so are your horses."

Virginia was sort of glad to agree to that, now that Brad and Red would be out to relieve her. She knew they could do much better and cover more territory than she had. As her dad had said, she was plenty tired, and now that the colts had been gone for so long, over a month, and she'd sort of lost hope of ever finding 'em she was resigned some and could rest a little easier.

Three and then four days wore on, and no sight of the riders. But she didn't fret so much, for she felt that as long as they was out and looking for the colts there'd still be hope.

But them two riders would have to be back on the next day wether they found the colts or not, for they'd have to be on their way again to take charge of the stock for another coming rodeo. Jim had been left to keep his eye on 'em in some pasture close by there.

Brad and Red did show up on the next day, late. So late that the ranch house was all dark. They was glad because they was tired, and would rather not tell of their failure in finding either track or hide of the colts until morning come, when they'd have to leave.

If they could of had another day or so they would of found 'em because they'd been combing around and in the badlands and had been close to where they was ranging. Brad and Red hardly thought they'd be there, but as horse hunters know, strayed stock is sometimes found where least expected, and they'd went but that'd took another day or two and added that much more time for their return, making them too late to handle the stock that'd been contracted for for the rodeo.

They would of told Virginia of the only country they hadn't rode when they talked to her the next morning as they was fixing to leave but that would be useless, they thought, and besides they might get another chance to ride that country some other time. They knew it was all rough and wild-horse country, it would take a lot of riding and time, and if the colts was there and had joined in with some wild bunch as it was naturally figured they would, well, it would take plenty more riding and time.

Virginia took the disappointment sort of calm, thanked Brad and Red for their efforts, bid 'em "good luck" as they got in the car and drove away, and then watching the car disappear in a cloud of dust, it seemed her last hopes sort of went with it.

As they left, Virginia didn't have much heart in even thinking of how to go on, if at all, in hunting for the colts. It seemed altogether useless and hopeless now, especially after them two so experienced horse hunters had failed, besides, she hadn't as yet received no word from the other neighboring riders who had and would be on the lookout for them. Then there'd been the many long days she'd spent and long weary miles she'd covered without one sign of 'em to encourage her in the hunting. It all proved very hopeless.

But in often thinking of 'em it was hard to give up and entirely lose hope of ever finding them. It was disappointing and aggravating enough with losing track of just plain range stock, but with them two little colts which she'd become so attached to. Well, it was much of another story.

Worrying about 'em as she sometimes did she thought of many things that might of happened to 'em, like getting down in bad places where they couldn't get up or out of. Maybe lions might of got 'em, for there was some which sometimes came from the badlands to the horse range. (She'd made a close guess there.) There was many other things she thought of which might of happened to the colts. One was so young and small and the other so green and helpless.

Likely hapepnings to them would crowd up in her mind until she could hardly stand it no more, then she'd go to the corrals, saddle one of her now rested horses and go for a ride, with her dad or at whatever stock work might need to be done, and then she'd get to thinking in more cheerful ways, that nothing could of happened to them colts, they was too strong and active, Charro was too wise, Colonel was too fast, and with the middle of summer now on, with good grass and water everywhere they would be just roaming around, enjoying their freedom, and sometime, when she'd least expect, she'd ride onto 'em.

Such thoughts was sort of cheering, and as she rode most every day, there wasn't only the work to keep her interested but also the steady looking for the runaways, with some returning hope that she would find 'em, maybe any day.

The summer wore on that way. Brad and Red didn't get to come to the ranch no more during that time, for rodeos in many different parts of the country came fast and steady and kept the boys on the jump. They wouldn't be able to return to the ranch until late fall, and then there'd be the rush of the fall round ups and works to be finished. There'd be no time for Brad and Red to go hunting for the colts no more that year unless a couple of extra riders was hired to take their place, and such riders who knew the country so well would be hard to find.

Virginia had of course notified the two line riders which her dad kept but their riding never took 'em anywheres near the wildhorse range, where the colts was running. As for Cal, himself, he seldom got very far away from the home ranch, for his interests and the

handling of the outfit was from there. But that summer
he did get away more than usual, not to go hunting for
the colts because, secretly, he didn't care if they was
found or not. He'd been thru with thoroughbreds, and
it was only for Virginia's sake that he sort of wished
they would be found.

So, seeming as tho that was hopeless, and wanting to
get her mind off of 'em, he'd framed up some excuses
to have her go with him to different places, in the car
and sometimes to be gone for quite a few days at a time,
at rodeos which she always enjoyed and also taking some
of her friends along for more company, for Cal would
most always want to be amongst stock and the company
of the men there.

But even tho she enjoyed herself during the trips,
she showed no enthusiasm when her dad would tell her
of going on one. She would be slow in getting ready,
for, leaving always reminded her of the time she did
leave for such trips and returned to find the colts gone.
Then she'd be all the more anxious to get back in the
saddle when returning, asking Anne and the boys at
the line camps if any word had been heard or any sign
had been seen of 'em. She'd sometimes even hope and
expect the colts to've been found during her absence,
and been put in the corral or pasture again.

The car wouldn't seem to go fast enough on the way
back, then only to be disappointed each time the ranch
was reached, for the colts wouldn't be in the corrals nor
pasture and there'd only be head shakings as to their
whereabouts when she'd inquire. Nobody had seen 'em.

CHAPTER EIGHT

THE RETURN OF THE PRODIGAL

BUT the colts had come mighty close to being seen by humans a couple of times that summer, and for a very short time, Charro had. Mustang runners had been swooping in on that range, and it'd been thru only Charro's watching, keeping in out of the way places and from joining any wild bunch that him and Colonel hadn't been rode onto and maybe run into traps with others.

, He'd often watched some long streaks of dust as bunches of wild ones would be heading up long ridges for the badlands, sometimes only to run into the wings of blind traps while trying to make their get away. At the first sight of such dusts, Charro was quick to lead the way to where him and Colonel could see but not be seen.

Colonel hadn't been much for hiding that way, especially sometimes when up on some high point and a good breeze would be fannng him. He couldn't understand, but, sensing Charro's warnings and knowing of his wisdom from past experiences, he would always follow.

But there'd been one time when Colonel couldn't follow. He'd got sick, so sick and weak that he could hardly navigate. It'd been from drinking from a pool where alkali from one spring and sulpher from another run together mixed and stilled. Charro hadn't drank any of that water but many wild horses had and with no bad effects, for there being much of that kind of water in the western ranges, the wild horse, like the range-bred horse, was well used to it.

But not so with Colonel, and this mixed pool he'd drank out of liked to layed him flat to stay. For a week or so afterwards he was moping around like hardly seeing, lost all his slim roundness and was in near as bad a shape as Charro had been when Brad found him after he'd lost his mother. Only Colonel wasn't suffering as Charro had, and he could realize a few things, but he couldn't follow Charro any distance and he didn't care to eat. But before he'd got too weak, Charro had managed to lead him on to another and more out of the way spring, too small for any bunch of horses to come to, and purer water, with only a little sulphur in this one.

It'd been there that Charro took his stand to watch over his sick and long legged pardner, and now that he was near a year old he could do a mighty fair job at that. He'd been grazing at a little distance one day, while Colonel was at his sickest, when he seen a rider coming straight his way, so close that he'd had no chance to duck out of sight. He suspicioned that rider to be a mustanger, and so, thinking fast, his wild instinct led him to act according. He'd hit out as tho a bunch of hornets had lit into him and kept a going that way up country, like towards the badlands, until he come to a tall pinnacle, which he circled soon as he lost sight of the rider, then on the other side of it, where he waited a spell to see if the rider would follow, and seeing no sign of him, started slowly back for a brushy hollow near the spring, where he'd left Colonel in hiding.

Charro's jumping out of the way he had did more than lead the rider away from the spring, for, seeing the lone yearling hit out that rider felt satisfied there'd been no more horses there, if there had they'd also showed themselves and run as the colt did.

As it was, the rider had followed on, not trying to catch up with the colt, for one lone one is not bothered with by mustang runners, besides, a bunch is easier handling, and at that time he'd seen the dust of a good sized bunch, one that some of his partners had spooked (started) and which he was to try to turn towards a trap, along with more that'd come.

But, if it hadn't been for Charro's play, Colonel would of been found. He of course couldn't of been moved right then, but seeing at a glance that Colonel was no mustang and well worth many of 'em, he'd been kept track of until he was on his feet again then brought into the mustanger's camp, taken care of and got in fair shape, when he'd been shipped along with mustangs and sold for what he'd be worth to a stranger, which would of put him in a worse fate than he'd ever been in, for no telling of who would of bought him or what he'd been put to.

Anyway, Charro hadn't wanted to lose his pardner, and when he got back, seen the mustanger off at a long

So close that he'd had no chance to duck out of sight

distance and fast riding way he drew a long breath of relief and went to the hollow where, stretched out to the sun, Colonel layed plum unaware of Charro's run in leading the mustanger off.

If Brad, or even Virginia had showed up at that time, or, for that matter, any time since Charro had got to his home range, they'd found him the same way the mustanger had, a very different acting colt from the one of only a month or so before. For as gentle as he'd been while at the ranch, every bit as tame as Colonel was, he'd now gone back to his natural wild state. What was inborn in him had sprouted to life with his returned strength, and now back in his wild surroundings he was the same as the mustangs or any other wild animal in that country, only wiser by his knowledge of the human's ways.

It wasn't ingratitude nor forgetfulness that'd changed Charro so, it was his natural and born-free instinct, like that of the eagle or wolf, and even tho maybe tame in captivity there was no resisting any chance to freedom.

He'd of a sudden tamed down again and well remember Virginia's good care if once caught. He'd et out of her hand and followed her around the same as Colonel would then, but now, being free was his life, and for as long as he could breathe it was in his blood to keep that freedom. No good care or treatment could take the place of that.

All animals have more or less that wild instinct, even *some* humans show it pretty strong and only are more greedy, cruel and ruthless. There's none of such in the wild horse, and even tho Charro was very different than Colonel that was due to the many generations of his ancestors having been left to rustle for their own feed and shelter thru the centuries before him. Charro's far back ancestors had come from as fine blood as Colonel's was, but in making their own in a wide, wild and mighty strange land they had to adapt themselves to fit it. It took many generations but by nature's hand and necessity, and as them first fine-bred horses accumulated, growed wild and spread from Mexico north during the centuries there wasn't much trace left of the built and looks of their great ancestors. They'd got smaller, narrower, but not in the brain, for they was very wise, wary and wiley, much quicker and hardier, and even tho they'd lost some of the speed they made up for that in every endurance to where their very own ancestors would be lost in trying to keep track of 'em.

Charro was one of just such descendents, and with the generations thru centuries of wild blood in his veins he was now, in comparison to Colonel, the same as a wolf to a great dane.

He'd showed his natural wild wisdom when he'd led Colonel to a good hiding place, then led the mustanger away from there afterwards. He'd also showed the spirit of his wild breed when, as Colonel was at his sickest and hadn't been able to get up for a couple of days, he'd fought off the cayotes that circled around and sensing Colonel's helplessness, would have soon attacked and put an end to him. Charro had stood guard night and day over him during that time, and even if lions had come, which they might of, he'd made a stand and, young as he was, would of most likely went down in fighting for his friend.

Colonel was sick for a couple of weeks and got down to a shadow, then, finally recovering, it took him still longer to recuperate enough so he could go on with Charro some more while grazing, sunning and watering. And there, with watering, was where he'd learned one more lesson which he'd never forget. That was to know the watering places, and when afterwards, Charro would pass on by a spring without touching of the water, Colonel would be sure to do the same, no matter how thirsty he might of been. There'd be bleached bones around such springs, like signs of how poisonous they was, and Colonel had got to know them by that. If he'd drank out of one of them springs instead of the sulphur and alkali pool as he had, his bones would of also now been bleaching with the others round there.

With the lessons Colonel had now learned and pulled thru by the help and coaching of Charro there was many more which was due to come his way. But he'd got by with about the worst ones, only now he'd have to watch out so them same experiences wouldn't repeat, in a different way.

Being on the alert always, sensing danger and signs of it from a breeze, quiet noises, sudden flight of a bird, a rolling stone or many such signs which warns all of the wild wasn't as yet known or even noticed by Colonel, and he would never learn to notice or under-

stand them much, not as long as he was with Charro.
For, depending as he'd got to on that little• wild one's
wisdom and alertness he was like blind to anything but
him and would near entirely depend, go or do by his
signals, which he now understood well.

To detect and learn all signs as Charro knew them
he would have to be by himself, and that would take a
long and dangerous time of hard learning, like with
the sureness of his footing and the steadiness of his long
legs in the rough and rocky country, he would never
be able to master that, not in *his* generation, nor for a
few after him. But this which he had gone thru and the
more that was to come would give him a mighty good
start.

His strength and roundness now sort of returned to
him, Charro took the lead as usual and now went on
more and more on the outskirts of his range, for along
about then the mustang runners was getting numerous
and there was seldom a day passed when the dust of
many bunches of wild horses stirred by them wasn't seen
streaking thru the country. Gradually, many bunches
started to migrate out of that range, some to maybe
return when the mustangers would let up for a time.

It was during such migrating that one day, Charro
finally decided to join one of the bunches. Him and
Colonel had made acquaintance with a couple of bunches
before, but for some being too ornery in one bunch, and
the most being "weedy" (locoed) in another they hadn't
gone with 'em very far, only to find 'em out.

There was only six in the bunch Charro finally figured

would be all right. Four of 'em was young stallions which had been whipped out of bunches by older ones, still too young to get and hold their own. A couple of years more and they would start making it interesting for them same or other stallions, and maybe whip 'em out of the same bunches they'd been whipped out of. The other two in the bunch was old reprobate saddle horses, one which had been caught from a wild bunch, well broke to ride, and then got away when his chance come, which was very natural. The other was a good range-bred horse, which had been too tough for one cowboy, bucked him off, run on packing the saddle for a spell when, after ganting up some, it slipped under his belly and he kicked it to pieces.

Them two ex-saddle horses made fine wise leaders and wasn't afraid of even the wicked fighting stallions of any bunches. All they'd keep shy of was the man on horseback, first, the lion which they only gave room to, second, and of course the rattler was respected too.

Charro had spotted that little bunch from a high ridge where him and Colonel had been breezing themselves, and he didn't have to move out of his tracks to see what they was, for as they trailed along slow they came to skirting right alongside of the ridge he was on and, without being seen, could make out that this wasn't a dangerous bunch. He started down to meet them, and Colonel, still leary from his first meeting with a bunch, watchfully followed, ready to backtrack to a flying run at the first threatening move from any of them.

The first of getting acquainted didn't take long, there

was just the ordinary squealing and pawing but no fighting, and the bunch went on, Charro and Colonel left to follow or not to, as they pleased.

They followed, and as they went on with 'em for a couple of days and got more acquainted, seen which one was first boss, second boss and so on, Charro sort of figured they would be a good bunch to range with, no bullies or trouble makers, and with the wise old leaders, even Charro could still learn plenty more. There wasn't a "dopey one" in the bunch.

With Charro finally deciding to join in with a bunch that way, it wasn't that he was any time lonesome with only Colonel or that he wanted more company, it was that in numbers there'd be a steadier watch kept, not all could be asleep at the same time, and of course the company would also be good, along with a feeling of more security. Colonel at least thought so, and after he got acquainted with all of 'em in turn, he grazed and travelled along by the side of any as well as he did with Charro.

But not for very long at a time, and when anything happened to set the bunch to looking up and around or spooked to a trot or a run he was right away by Charro's side again.

There was more running since joining the bunch than there'd been when the two was alone, and the reason was that, with Charro, he'd been more for watching from high points and only to hiding, where he could still watch when such as a rider would be sighted. The only time he ever would hide.

The bunch was'nt much for hiding, but more for high-tailing it at the sight of a rider or the far away dust of a running bunch, winding along thru rough and deep cuts and canyons and sometimes at full speed on some high ridges or open lands where they'd be in sight of the rider for a spell and while hitting for some more rough country.

Colonel more than enjoyed them running spurts, much more than Charro and the other wild ones did, for, with him, there was no fear of riders nor worry in getting away from them. He run more like for the fun of it and of course to keep with his pal, Charro and the bunch, and there was times, when all was running at their best, they would still be too slow for him and he'd come up to run with the leaders. Sometimes he'd run past and away ahead of them, but then he wouldn't follow his lead, which wouldn't be a wise one, and he would have to turn to get in with it again.

But there come one time when, even tho by accident, his lead had turned out to be a wise one. But the bunch hadn't followed him, none but Charro, when a rider swooped down on the bunch and to going where he wanted it to go, towards a blind trap.

Seeing that the bunch wasn't following, Colonel was for turning to catch up with 'em as he'd done before, not at all minding nor realizing what the sight of the fast coming rider meant. But Charro, now being with him, once again took the lead, right on the way Colonel had started and away from the bunch.

At that, Colonel hesitated and near stopped while half

ways between Charro and the bunch, wondering which to
go with. But there was no wondering for long as he once
again looked the direction of his little pardner making
mighty good speed and now all alone. The bunch
wouldn't be much without him.—With a shake of his
head, and acting as wild as any of the wild ones he'd
seen and been with, he then raised it high, snorted near
as good as a wild one would, throwed up his tail, sort of
bounced along like an antelope for a ways and then
stretched out to his top speed, to soon catch up with
Charro.

Colonel had put on such a speed in catching up with
Charro that the mustang runner, even tho mighty busy
watching and riding hard after the remaining six of the
bunch, couldn't help but notice the speed of the dark,
long legged yearling. He'd never seen any such before,
not even amongst some mighty fast and grown wild ones.
And that made him wonder, not only at the speed of him
but for what he might be. For there was well bred horses
would sometimes get away and join the wild ones. Sometimes, also, the studs would "steal" mares from the gent-
ler and better bred range stock bunches.

The mustanger glanced at him in admiration a couple
of times more, and if it hadn't been that the six horses
he was chasing looked good to him, knowing, even from
the long distance, that at least four of 'em was young
studs, which are always the pick to mustang runners,
he'd of left the six go and went after the two bunch quit-
ters, Colonel and Charro.

He of course knew that, even with the fast horse he

was riding, he wouldn't have no chance to catch up with
or turn that dark streak of speed, but he somehow felt
that that dark colt, with all his speed, wouldn't be as
hard to manage as the light colored one he was with. He'd
noticed that the dark one didn't act like the wild ones and
was running only not to be left behind, that he didn't
show no fear of him and wouldn't make a break as a regular wild one would when crowded. He didn't figure he'd
leave the light colored one, and that one could be hazed
into a trap, the mustanger thought, for he didn't have
the speed.

But right then, and being the six horses ahead was
running well and in the direction he wanted 'em to, he'd
stay with them, on to the wings of the trap and where a
couple of other mustangers would join him and help run
'em on in. He would get after that fast one and his pardner on the next day.

But them two didn't seem to be nowheres in or around
that country on the next day. The mustanger, as wise
as he was to the wild ones' ways, had got fooled, and by
the also wise little Charro. Him and Colonel had left no
tracks as to their going on, and that was simple enough,
even tho seldom done, but they hadn't gone on. Charro
had stopped soon as the mustanger and the bunch had
disappeared, then, instead of going on and making a circle as most wild horses would of done, he'd turned and
backtracked right from there, and his and Colonel's trail
was soon mixed with others of that same day. There was
no fresh trail of two colts to follow and to make it still
better for them and harder on the mustanger, they run

onto two renegade saddle horses to mix their trail with
and go on to other ranges.

Them two renegades being wise to traps and sort of
sensing that, on account the rider hadn't tried to turn
'em during the run, all going too well, for him, and when
they quit the bunch and he tried to turn 'em back they
knew then they was getting away. They went against and
past him, leaving the four young studs which he'd managed to keep going on, on into the trap.

Them four now made as wise a small bunch as there
was in that wild horse country, all excepting one, and
that one made up with speed for the wisdom he lacked.
He sure didn't need to be waited for, and with them three
wise ones to learn from he might, in years, turn out to be
a fair leader. If he ever got a bunch that would and could
follow him he'd soon lead 'em on to freedom, or into a
trap.

But there was few mustangers where the four trailed
on to from the time they got together after the chase,
and as luck, or fate, would have it it was towards the country where Brad had found Charro a year or so before.
Charro sort of remembered some of the country, where
he'd tried to follow his mother while her and the bunch
was being chased. They didn't get as far as where he'd
had to quit but near there, and now, as him, Colonel and
the two renegades went to ranging in that country, he
felt that he was still on his home range, at least along
the trail and not so far from where he'd last seen his
mother.

The range the four had picked on was a little out of

the wild horse country, where there was more good water, grass and shelter, lions was scarcer and there was no blind traps, for few mustangs ever came there on account it was more of a cow country and where there of course was more riders. It was a country sort of between wild horse and cow country, where the cattle also got pretty wild and sometimes the riders would have to pack a rifle along with their rope to get 'em down out of the rough mountain ranges.

Being there was so few and scattering little bunches of wild horses in that country the riders that came there seldom was out to get them. These riders would be after cattle, and being that mustang running and cattle gathering don't mix, also that if mustangs was wanted they'd go where they was more plentiful, the few wild ones in that country was left pretty well alone. But they had to be very wise ones, wiser than the average wild one or they'd get caught there too. The two renegades and Charro was plenty wise that way, wise enough to know the difference between a rider that's after cattle and the one that's out especially to get the mustang.

To Colonel, every rider was the same, just a man on a horse and nothing to be afraid of. But he did like to run, along with the three wise ones. The only time that bothered him was when his three pardners would "spook" at the sight of some rider and, regardless of where they was, would light out, sometimes more like falling than running off the steep and rough mountain sides, over down timber and thru thick brush as tho it was all smooth bridle paths. At the sight of a rider is when they would take to such country, the rougher the better, and there was where Colonel would often hesitate and sometimes to be left away behind, when he would then take big chances, and some falls, for his legs and breeding wasn't for such lands, and even tho he somehow managed he was often much worried until open and more level stretches was reached.

Being an intelligent colt he realized the handicap of his long legs and slim ankles and that saved him many a fall, maybe a broken neck or leg, for he'd learned not to go headlong into dangerous places, more and more with getting snagged now and again, skinned up with scraping along sharp ledge rock, dead limbs as stiff and dangerous as bayonets, even to vines that would tangle him up and sometimes throw him. But the worse for him was to climb up the places his pardners would, so steep and high that it would even bother a mountain goat. Coming to such places, Colonel would get to do a lot of watching and some tall figuring to get around, and being there'd seldom be any other way he'd have to tackle it or stay behind, for none of the three but maybe Charro would wait for him.

But such runs and rough goings on being not too frequent, Colonel had a chance to sort of recuperate in between each and getting wiser and surer of footing right along, for being young he had a good chance to grow into that, and, as it was, after that summer and from the start with Charro he would now be too much for a grown one of his own breed to follow, unless that one was raised in that country as Colonel was being.

Late fall come with Colonel still going strong, and even tho scarred and scratched up some there was a twinkle in his eyes that hadn't been there some months before, the blank greenhorn look was gone and now when he looked at a thing it was direct and with more understanding. Even his appearance had changed some and there wasn't so much of that helpless rooky look about him. And he could now more than ever pass any animal on that range, when on a level stretch.

The four was well up in the mountains when the first big snow of the year come. It fell to more than four feet at the timber line, and then's when Colonel got to see some of the animals he'd been on the same range with. There was elk, mountain sheep and deer begin to come down from the high country and deep snows and heading for the foothills. The horses was already there, ahead of the storm and would be hitting on for still lower country as more storms would come, but no lower than would be possible.

The storms came, near like on the heels of one another, and so that the horses not only had to get down off the mountains but from the foothills and at the edge of the big flats. Colonel again felt more at ease along the rolling lands but there was no advantage to that much now, for the snow being so deep even there he couldn't very well run. Lunging and slow walking was about all he could do, and after now having to paw deep for his grass or brush he didn't feel any like running. That energy went to pawing for more feed which was scarce there and couldn't near get enough of. What was more there was very little shelter in the bleak and open country, and the snow was too deep to get where there was some. The feed was also beyond pawing for there.

The first big snow came in late that year, much later than it had the fall before, but when it did come it didn't let up and go to chinooking as it had then. It stayed and piled on steady, and when it finally let up some to fine particles cold winds came to drift it into deep banks, bared the land a little where there was no feed, to cover up the most of what there was.

It was the start of a hard winter, with no let up, when much stock and game would be snowbound and many would starve. Riders would be at their busiest in all kinds of such weather, breaking trails and freeing snowbound stock. They would have no time to run mustangs even if they was right in their way, and the wise renegades with Charro and Colonel knew it. They got so they would roam and feed where they felt like and didn't run much any more at the sight of a rider in the distance.

In roaming the barren country that way, now steady in search of feed, the four had got into the valley where now over a year before the Hip O wagon had made camp and Charro had rode in it to the ranch from there. And now, even tho from another angle, Colonel realized he wasn't so far from the ranch, and there was no badlands between, for them had been gone around. And now, with old man winter steady holding his grip the brown colt, getting lean and gant, often looked the direction of the ranch and tried to lead the bunch on to that direction.

Charro would sometimes look up that way too and

would follow along while pawing for the scarce feed, but never for very far from the two renegades which wasn't for leaving the mountains too far behind and crossing the big valley, not towards no ranch, no matter how hard the winter nor how scarce the feed.

If Charro would of only followed, Colonel would of been quick to've now taken the lead and on back to the ranch, even to leaving the two older horses, but there was no leading Charro from them nor that direction, for even tho he'd still rather have the company of his pal, Colonel, and would have went on with him he wouldn't go the direction of the ranch than any wild horse would. A deer or an elk might, for the hay they would maybe get, but not a wild horse, and Charro had gone back to that stage.

The deep snow, scarce feed and cold didn't tell on him or the other two as it did on Colonel. With them, they only lost some of their summer belly and roundness but was strong as before and wasn't as yet ganted up nor lean as Colonel was. Besides their hides was thicker, the veins not so close to the surface and their hair was thicker, and longer, waving like tall grass to the wind, where, with Colonel, his hair wasn't much longer than it'd been the summer before and looked like he'd shed off in comparison with the others' long shaggy coats. The severe cold was as much the cause of his shrinking and ganting up as the scarcity of feed, and it was no wonder he looked sort of longingly the direction of the ranch. There'd be warmth there, good clover and blue stem hay, and even warm water to drink.

As the severe cold and wind kept up it was also a wonder why he didn't go back there, even if alone, but a horse being more attached to one another than any other animal he hadn't wanted to leave Charro, not even for the comforts he knew awaited him at the ranch.

Then old man winter took a hand, blasted him with hard stinging snow and cold winds that chilled him to the bone. And, as old man winter would have it the first and sudden cold blasts of that storm hit him as he was quite a distance from Charro, which he'd been sort of trying to coax to follow, and with the suddenness of the blinding snow that come he couldn't make it back to him. He tried but he was near like a tumble weed against that wind and he was forced to put his rump to it and only stand. Charro, being in some shelter with the others, nickered for him but the whistling wind killed the sound, and not realizing but what Colonel was also in shelter somewhere close he didn't budge, for he knew there was no use looking for him in that storm.

Colonel, now all alone, in a bleak opening and where the storm had a clean sweep at him, stood with rump to the storm, head down and moving one leg and then another up and down in the whirling snow to sort of keep circulation. But that didn't help and he was fast getting numb, so that he could hardly move his legs anymore. And he hardly cared, for soon, the cold feeling and suffering begin to leave him and now he was beginning to feel warm, comfortable and sleepy. That was the first stage of freezing.

And, but for being now sort of hardened to the steady

Now all alone, in a bleak opening and where the storm had a clean sweep at him

cold, he fould have froze where he stood. He would have any way but, like without realizing, he begin to move a little, to move with the wind, and that seeming to relieve him some from standing against it he moved on some more, very slow at first but steadier as he went on, to finally drifting along with the storm and losing all sense that he was drifting on alone.

The storm kept him a drifting on thru the whole long night that way, and being he was now in the big open valley, where there was no breaks nor timber for shelter he was sort of swept along, thru drifts, and there was no stopping to paw for feed in the blinding white sheeted land, no stopping until the storm did or he couldn't go no more.

It was along near the middle of the next day when the storm and wind finally sort of let up, so did Colonel, and when he could now see a little he found he hadn't been the only one to drift, for, not so far ahead was a dark line of what looked like stock, and sort of encouraged at the sight he moved on some more, towards that line. It was cattle.

Cattle that had drifted on until they couldn't drift further. For they'd come to a fence where, with humped backs, they lined up to wait for the end of the storm, and there among 'em, is where Brad and another rider, while checking up on the cattle, found Colonel that day, also all humped up, but showed a very good spark of life as the sound of the surprised cowboy's voice came to his ears.—The prodigal had returned.

CHAPTER NINE

NOBODY'S HORSE

IT WASN'T no triumphant nor proud home coming for Colonel, and like most prodigals he'd come home to eat, sleep and find shelter. At the sound of Brad's voice he'd nickered his gladness and after him and the other cowboy had picked out some weak stock that'd drifted along the fence and started 'em on towards the feed grounds near the ranch, Colonel made sure he didn't lose track of neither of the riders as they worked thru the cattle, cut out the weak ones and started 'em on, and he didn't need no leading as he followed them and the cattle thru a gate and on towards the ranch. He didn't have much strength, and with drifting on thru the storm, with very little feed and only snow to lap up for moisture during the past month or so of cold and snowy weather more than told on him. But now knowing of what all there would be for him once at the ranch, the thoughts of that is what kept him a going, following the riders, along with the lean and shaggy cattle. Not a very proud looking procession.

There was no sign that Colonel had been running free and amongst wild ones all that summer and fall past. None by his actions at least. Only his looks and condition he was in showed some signs of that. There was the plain scar along the back of his neck and which was a mark of one of his experiences. There was of course

174

quite a few other scratches and "barked" (pealed) places along his now thin frame but he was still all together, much the wiser, but with no show of any wild spirit, that he was inclined to make any break for freedom and try to be a wild one again, not for the time anyway. And as the ranch was reached and he followed Brad into the familiar box stall, was handed the cream of hay, warm water to drink, right in the warmth and shelter of the long log stable and amongst other horses he even didn't think of his little pardner Charro, who, at the time, was humped up in scanty shelter against the storm which was howling some more and showed no sign of letting up.

It had let up some during the day as Colonel had drifted in with the cattle but had come on full force again before dark. But Colonel didn't feel any of it, for there was a good thick wall of logs between him and that weather. He et and drank his fill then stretched and slept on the dry bedding of waste hay, his mouth and muscles sometimes twitching, like maybe dreaming of going over scary places in following Charro and the two renegades.

It had been a great spell of wild freedom for Colonel but old man winter and hunger had put an end to that like nothing elso could, and he was glad to get back to human care and comfort. He didn't mind the enclosures, inside walls nor fences, for, like the tame canary whose home is his cage, he was content and only very helpless outside of such. Without the lead and coaching of Charro, Colonel would of never lived thru his spell of that freedom, it wasn't in him to go wild or ever want to be away from the company of humans, not unless

maybe after years of steady wild freedom, and that
would have to be sort of forced on him thru circum-
stances.

With charro, being of wild blood, his freedom meant
much more to him than all the care any human could
give him. He'd rather go hungry, thirsty, buck all weather, all and everything at its worse than to be inside
any enclosure and be at the command and dependent of
the human. And now, while bumped against the cold
wind and storm, scarce feed under deep snow all aswirl-
ing white and blinding around him he had no thought
nor hankering for the good shelter and care of the winter before, that which had saved his life. He only thought
of the enclosures of that time, and that was against his
nature.

As Colonel was enjoying the comfforts of his warm
stall, so was Charro bearing well under the hardships of
his freedom. The little wild horse had no thought that his
long legged pardner had drifted on with the storm and
left him, he'd figured him in some shelter close by and
would find him soon as the storm let up and he could
see some distance again. It was impossible while the storm
blowed on, and he done well to even see the two older
horses which he'd sheltered within only a few feet of when
the storm hit so sudden.

It was still storming hard on the morning after Colonel's return to the ranch but that blue blood didn't know
anything about it until the stable door was swung open
and a gust of the cold wind hit him. The door was soon

closed and then he heard a familiar voice, Virginia's—.
Brad had told her that morning that a hat rack covered
over with a horse hide had sneaked in there the night
before and she'd ought to go see about it.

She of course knew by Brad's pleased grin at the telling what the "hat rack" might be, and even tho she
hadn't had her breakfast as yet that could wait, and she
wasted no time getting down to the stables, to find the
blinking, lean and shaggy Colonel.

If there ever was any thought in anyone's mind of
punishing or scolding a wayward runaway that was the
last thing that could come to Virginia's at her glad surprise of seeing the colt again, and being so thin and weak
looking drawed only deep sympathy. She now only
thought more of him for his returning of his own accord
and would be very happy to give him the best of care and
put him back in shape. That would give her great
pleasure.

She was nearly too happy and excited with Colonel's
return to take time to come back to the house and eat her
breakfast, but not to keep her dad and Anne waiting
she finally rushed back, and then she was calmed down
some by her dad asking, "What about Charro?"

With her excitement at again seeing Colonel, little
Charro hadn't come to her mind. That is, she'd been so
surprised and pleased that for the time she couldn't think
of anything else but Colonel. But now that she'd been
reminded of the little wild colt it come sudden as to how
strange he wasn't along too, for they'd been such close
pals and wouldn't separate, not unless something where

one just couldn't follow the other. It would have to be something very serious, she thought.

Telling her dad of her fears that way only made him grunt and grin as he waved a hand at such fears. "Don't you worry about that little fuzztail," he says, "you'll find him bucking high and slick as an eel when that mosquito-built, brown wind-cutter of yours would be folding up. It's just that he didn't want to come back and be fussed over, and I'll bet he'll do as well right wherever he is as Colonel will in the stable, by the mangerful of the good feed he doesn't have to rustle for."

"I hope you're right, Dad." Virginia said, "but I wish he'd returned too. Him and Colonel had so much fun playing together."

"Yeh, but I wouldn't worry about him. Besides, some of the boys might run acrost him any time. I've an idea Colonel was with him and not very far away or he wouldn't of left him to come back here alone. He's with some bunch, along the edge of the valley somewhere and below the deep snow."

Cal didn't know how close he'd guessed, but that was it and from his knowledge and experience with horses. That guess also sounded reasonable to Virginia and relieved her of much worry about the little wild one. She felt too that, as her dad had said, the bows might run acrost him any time.

That happened sooner than was expected. It had stayed stormy and cold for a week after Colonel had returned, then as it cleared and got some warmer and the boys got to making bigger circles from the ranch and

He's with some bunch, along the edge of the valley somewhere
and below the deep snow

camps, Brad and Red, riding together one day, rode
onto three horses which had been hard at pawing for
their feed on the sunny side of a foothill. It was the two
renegades and little Charro.

Busy pawing as they'd been the horses didn't see the
riders until they'd topped the foothill, to within about
fifty yards. But at that it was an even break, for the
riders hadn't 'seen 'em no sooner, and right then there
soon got to be much more distance separating.

But at a glance and while the horses had stood sort
of petrified for a split second, Brad and Red had right
away recognized little Charro with the other two, and
they also being as surprised as the horses had been, just
sat, held their horses still and watched the three go,
Charro now as wild as the other two.

The boys hadn't been prepared for such a surprise,
and even tho they'd been on the lookout for Charro they
didn't think that him nor any other wild ones would be
so close to the ranch, only to within half a day's slow
riding, and they'd been more to watch for weak stock
amongst the scattered bunches of cattle than they had
for horses.

As luck would have it there was no cattle found that
needed taking in that day, the weaker ones had been
brought in right along until there was no more for the
time from that part of the range, and the two riders
had been about to circle back towards the ranch when
they'd run onto Charro.

Surprised as they'd been to see him they wasn't at all
surprised to see how wild he'd got. He'd be near as hard

to catch as the two renegades he was with. But as they sat on their horses and watched the three go they figured that now was the time to get him, while the snow was deep, maybe a little weak and before he'd get back to the wild horse range.

It would be very different in getting him than it had been with Colonel. The thoroughbred had been mighty glad to see the riders and follow them on in but the little wild one would have to be roped and being he wasn't broke to lead and wouldn't at all follow he'd have to be hazed on in at the end of the end of the rope.

It was good they'd just held their horses still and let the three run on. For one thing they hadn't been prepared and another they wanted 'em to have their first run. They wouldn't go far in the deep snow, and by the right kind of manouvering they could soon enough get to 'em from the right direction and at the right time. Against hardened, grain fed and fast saddle horses of the two cowboys little Charro wouldn't have much chance, the two older ones could maybe be caught too but them wasn't wanted, just little Charro.

The riders didn't move their horses until the wild ones got out of sight over another foothill ridge, then getting the general direction of their going they started further up and above 'em, more up towards the mountains, for it was figured there's where they'd hit for soon as the riders came to sight, and there, with the wild ones crowding to get by during the run, is where the good chance would come to get to within roping distance without having to do too much running.

It worked out as the riders figured, and they didn't hit out on a high lope to get to point above 'em, for the snow was too deep for one thing and another was the wild ones wouldn't go very fast either on that account nor very far before they'd stop.

The riders didn't have to go much over a couple of miles when they spotted the three wild ones again, now going only at a walk. But at the sight of the riders they started to run some more and up for the mountains, for the wise old renegades didn't care for the big flat below, too much open, and then's when the riders now had the leverage on 'em for they was already above and it would take quite a bit of the wild ones' wind to get there and past 'em.

But they tried it and there was a lunging run of over a mile when the riders a ways above the wild ones kept abreast of 'em. Then the wild ones begin to crowd to get up in the mountains and then's when the riders made their loops ready. Little Charro showed signs of being winded some, but he was game and wasn't far behind.

There was plenty of strength and speed in the hardened saddle horses of the two riders, and when the right time come, while the wild ones had got into deep drifts to get past and up in the mountains, they spurted their horses on and after a few seconds of scrambling in the deep snow, Brad's loop settled over Charro's head and around his neck. Red couldn't resist but make a throw at one of the renegades then, but he didn't try very hard and his loop fell short a couple of feet.

He didn't try no more, for Charro was the only one

that was wanted, and now, as Brad's loop drawed around his neck that little feller went against it and squealed like a regular wild one. He didn't want nothing to do with that rope nor recognize the human that'd caught him, and he was all for fighting that hemp that held him.

But there was no use of his doing that, and Brad only had to grin some in a way as he let him fight for a spell.

"Now, little feller," he says to the wild eyed Charro, "that aint no way for you to act, not even if your ma and pa and your great-great-grand ancestors was all wild ones. Do you forget the good treatment you had last winter and the pretty lady who took care of you and brought you back to life?—You ought to be ashamed of yourself."

"Yes," Red chipped in, also grinning "and you'd only get caught anyhow, sooner or later, and you wouldn't have the good home we're taking you back to. Then again, you might only get shot in the long run and be left for the cayotes to clean up."

But little Charro couldn't understand and wasn't in no mood to listen to any talk. The only thing he'd understood and appreciated right then would of been to had that rope slip off his neck and left to go and join the two renegades which had gone on, to their freedom.

The first useless and fighting spasm over, Charro quieted down some. He knew he was licked, and when Brad got off his horse and came towards him he hardly flinched, for he did remember that only gentle treatment had come from the touch of the human hand, so far, and even tho he didn't hanker for any such right then he seen

Brad's loop settled over Charro's head and around his neck

where he sort of had to resign himself and be the gentle colt he had the winter before.

He didn't flinch nor try to jerk away now as Brad tied a hackamore with the rope and slipped it over his head, and even tho he wasn't broke to lead as Colonel had he soon enough seen he was to follow the way that rope pulled him as Brad got back on his horse and started for the ranch, for Red was riding close behind him and with a flip of the end of his rope on his rump would keep him from pulling back.

And so, as Colonel's return wasn't at all triumphant nor proud while following shaggy and weak cattle to the ranch, neither was Charro's, for he was being taken back like a prisoner, an outlaw, one rider ahead and pulling him with a rope and another behind to see that he didn't hang back on that rope.

It was slow travelling and late that night when the two riders pulled into the ranch with their "prisoner" and put him in the same box stall with the now well fed and good feeling Colonel, that long legged pardner of his. And being with him again was the only thing that sort of helped at that time, once again in captivity.

When the next morning come and Virginia was told there was another parcel wrapped in horse hide for her at the stable, that it didn't look so much like a hat rack as the first one had and so on, it again didn't take her long to guess what that parcel was, nor getting down to the stable to see it.

Charro recognized Virginia as quick as Colonel had, and now was as gentle as he'd been wild only the morning before. Once tamed a wild horse seldom ever forgets, and even tho he might get away and run wild again the catching of him is the hardest, harder than catching one that'd never been caught or tamed, but once caught again he'll soon come back to all that's been taught him in the taming. But he'll always get away every chance he gets if kept near the country where he was raised and caught. There's no breaking him from that natural instinct.

It was the same with Charro. He didn't grieve so much at being caught and kept closed in again, not near as much as a full grown wild one would, for sometimes some of them are so broken hearted they won't eat while inside an enclosure and will finally die.

With Charro having spent his first winter in the stable and corrals made it some easier for him this second time, and with the company of Colonel and no humans to fear now that that there was no freedom to watch out and run for so's to keep he sort of made the best of it, and especially that it was winter, cold and stormy, the good hay, warm shelter and water was sort of welcome, for that time. Only, not to be able to go where and when he pleased, to be faced by heavy log walls and corral bars wherever he turned was like being in prison, that sort of chafed, sometimes more than it had that first winter, for now he'd had a good taste of the freedom that was inborn in him, and he couldn't come to realize that such wasn't to be no more.

But still being mighty young, not yet a year and a half old, getting the best of care and feeling mighty good he'd at times forget his being in captivity and go to playing with Colonel in the big corral in near the same way as that thoroughbred would, also to following Virginia around again the same as he had the winter before, when she'd come to visit, feed or water 'em.

The winter wore on that way, kind of slow for Charro, but being it was so furious and steady with wind, cold and snow he took to the barred enclosures, warm shelter and good hay with a near contented feeling. But an opened gate, even during the worst of the weather, would of been more than welcomed. He'd again been quick to hit out, been harder than ever to find or get near and it would again took a rope to bring him back.

With the coming of spring there was more and more the restless feeling of roaming with him. He'd got to walking around and round the big corral like a lion in a cage, stop to gaze at the greening hills once in a while, at the distant badland ridges and all around and wouldn't eat much. There was no more play in him by then, and when the much contented and good feeling thoroughbred would sometimes tear loose into one of them spells he seemed to hardly notice him and would only put his ears back or kick at him when Colonel would nip at him in trying to get him to play too. He was in no mood for any such nonsense.

Virginia got to noticing that, and more too was that he wouldn't come near nor follow her around like he had, and when Colonel would come to her as usual he'd got to staying by himself or just walking around the corral and looking outside it, hardly seeming to notice her or Colonel.

As Brad would again sometimes come to the corrals to visit with Virginia of evenings, talking about the colts and things in general he also got to noticing Charro's restless acting.

"That little feller is getting poor too," he once said as he watched him pacing back and forth in the corral. He ought to be picking up instead, with all the good feed you've been giving him the past months."

"Maybe he will when I turn him and Colonel out in the pasture." Virginia said. "I think he has the spring fever," she laughed, "and it's green grass he wants."

"More than that" grinned Brad. "It's them far away hills he's hankering for, his freedom, and if I was you I'd be sure to add on a pole all around the top of the whole pasture fence before he's turned in there or he might make a break out of it."

Virginia also thought that would be a wise thing to do, and when she told her dad he at first didn't see no sense of going to the trouble of topping the pasture fence with a pole all around, not for only a little wild horse when he already had so many well bred ones.

"Why don't you just let the poor little devil go?" he said. "He don't want to be cooped up in no pasture anyway."

"But he's young and might get over that. Besides, Colonel would sure miss him, and if I turned the two out together and Charro broke away Colonel would be sure to follow."

"All right," Cal had finally grunted. "I don't know

which one is the most trouble, that spindle-legged thoroughbred or the sawed-off wild one."

Anyway, and within a couple of days, a string of peeled, lodge pine poles was strung and pegged along the top of the pasture fence, making it not only a good looking fence but a hard one to get thru or over. It was five foot high, and a fox hunting horse could of easy cleared it if in mind to but not Charro, not unless he was crowded, and then he'd be more apt to go thru it instead.

But there'd be no crowding him, and when him and Colonel was turned out in that pasture it looked like it would sure enough hold him, if the gate was kept closed. Virginia asked her dad to warn all the ranch help as to that.

Charro again took the lead out of the corral into the pasture and the first place he'd hit for, on a high lope, was the gate at the other end and where he'd got out the summer before. But it was of course very well closed, and then, satisfied of that and sizing up the fence with top pole all around he went to nibbling at the green grass. That helped ease him some, and now he sort of felt he'd have to be contented and make the best of it, in the second best and closest he'd get to freedom, at least until there'd come another opening which he'd always be on the lookout for.

With the few saddle horses in the same pasture, Charro got to losing his restlessness as he grazed along with them and Colonel. As the days went by and there was no sign of his wanting to break out and begin to rounding out in good shape again, Virginia, then satisfied, decided it was a good time to start to work on some plans she had for Colonel. That was to train and break him to saddle.

Colonel was now a two year old. Her dad had told her that thoroughbreds was started in training and rode some when much younger than that, and being Colonel looked so fit, had shed off slick, was fat as his kind could get and now as tall as the grown saddle horses he was with it was high time something should be done with him, or started.

But what to do with him, what to start him at and for what purpose sort of had Virginia stumped. She didn't want and had no use for no ordinary, fancy or gaited "riding horse," no matter how pretty or easy riding he might be. She didn't know anything about race horses or how to train one, she didn't have any use for such either, and so it came about that, as Brad and her was in the pasture and looking at him one evening she asked him on the subject. She still carried the feeling that Colonel was partly his, for even tho he'd given her a clear bill of sale of him she'd still felt that way, then when she'd lost him, and after near giving up all hope of ever seeing him again, Brad had found him and brought him back to her. Anyway, she wanted his advice and felt he sure deserved some say as to what should be done with him.

But Brad didn't feet that way and was on guard the minute she started on the subject. For, remembering how she'd felt the spring before, how the colt wasn't all hers and the discussions there'd been over that, he was very

There was a kind of a queer grin on Brad's face, too, as he watched her walk away

careful and neutral so that that wouldn't repeat as the subject came up.

"Well," he says, as he got the drift of what she wanted of him, "I wouldn't know just what to suggest.—He's *your* horse, you know, and you better do with him as you see fit your own self. If I was to suggest anything I'd most likely be wrong in the long run, and that wouldn't do."

Virginia was set back quite a bit at the kind of refusal, and she could tell right away what had caused it. She appreciated it in a way, and then again she felt hurt, hurt that he wouldn't have nothing to say or do with the training of the colt. He'd helped her with her other horses when she'd started breaking 'em, even topped 'em off for her when there was too much buck in 'em. But with this thoroughbred it was different and a kind of touchy proposition, like as any good intentions might turn to harm, and he figured it best to let well enough alone.

The talk came to an end sort of sudden on the subject. The two was silent for a spell, looking at the colt but hardly seeing him. Then, with a queer little smile and some kind of remark that she had to help Anne at something or other, Virginia started back for the house.

There was a kind of a queer grin on Brad's face, too, as he watched her walk away, and then looking at Colonel again he rubbed the colt's knowledge bump a bit and he said, to himself as much as to him,

"It'll be all right, old boy—I hope."

CHAPTER TEN

SADDLE AND BRANDING IRON

AS THE spring works was now in full swing and Cal and his riders was away on the outskirts of the Hip-O range for many days at a time it was near a week before Brad returned to the ranch, since that evening when him and Virginia has had that cool little tiff over Colonel, and it was Red who'd first spotted some results of that, for pinned to the log wall and by Brad's bunk was the bill of sale he'd made to Virginia for Colonel and on the same sheet by her own writing was added on: "I thank you but I don't want him." It was signed, Virginia.

With Red's laughing at the plain in sight sheet of writing, Brad was soon by his side, and after reading Virginia's added on writing he laughed too, but very little.

Red soon quit laughing too, but not before he had to remark how Colonel now seemed to be an unwanted colt, saying that if nobody wanted him he'd sure like to have him.

Brad didn't seem to hear him. Virginia didn't come down to the pasture that evening. That night he added on a few words to her writing and would give it to Anne to give to her before he'd start out for anther day's ride early the next morning. Brad's writing was short and to the effect that he wouldn't want the colt either, not now. That he was still all hers as far as he was concerned and to do with it as she seen fit.

There was no answer to that and the bill of sale with the added writing wasn't returned again, but Virginia wasn't seen down the pasture with the colt of evenings no more either, at least not while Brad was at the ranch, and it wasn't until sometime later, as Brad and Red and

Pinned to the log wall and by Brad's bunk was the bill of sale he'd made to Virginia for Colonel and on the same sheet by her own writing was added on: "Thank you. I don't want him." It was signed, Virginia

Jim run in the rodeo stock and made ready to hit out
for the first rodeo of the year that she sort of came out
of her hiding and told Brad how ashamed she was for the
way she'd acted and that she'd again take care of the
Colonel as usual while he was gone, but not a word did
she say about the bill of sale or her feelings as to the colt
being hers, nor of Brad refusing to have any say about
him.

But taking a chance and thinking it would make her
happy he told her to go ahead and start riding him, that
he might surprise her and maybe take to working cattle
better than might be expected. If he didn't he would
maybe suggest another scheme, if she wished. Brad had
sort of given in with this little show of interest in the
colt's training but he'd figured if it done any harm it
wouldn't be no worse than it had been since he'd refused
to have a word to say on the subject.

As it was, Virginia was glad to again take heart with
some plans for the colt. Of course what Brad had said,
to start and try him out at range work, wasn't much of
a lead to go by, but the scheme he spoke of if that didn't
do was what appealed to her. In the meantime she would
start riding him and see how he would take to a little
range work.

Brad and the other cowboys was no more than gone
with the bucking stock one early morning when Virginia
was down in the pasture, walked partways as Colonel
came to meet her and putting a rope around his neck,
led him up to the corrals and stables. Charro looked on,
kind of wondering, and followed for a ways, but when

nearing the corral gate he stopped, nickered once as Colonel was led in the stable and then went back to join the saddle horses he'd been grazing with. He'd sort of figured there was something up that wouldn't be to his liking.

Virginia was some surprised that the little grulla wouldn't follow. She wanted him in too, to keep Colonel company and from getting nervous. So she seen where she just had to go out and get him, but it took a pan of grain before he'd let her walk up to him and put a rope around his neck, for he was no more the little Charro of the winter before. All independent and not caring no more for human favors nor company.

But Colonel, he was still the same as ever before, kind and gentle and as always welcoming the sound of human voice or touch of hand. There'd be no *breaking* of him to riding or for anything else wanted of him to be done; it would all be only training and plain teaching, no bucking or fighting to get out of his system and no treacherous tricks for the rider to watch out for, not for the time anyway, nor never, unless he was aggravated into developing a mean streak, as sometimes is with some thoroughbreds.

If there'd been any danger or doubt as to Colonel's behaving, Brad would have wanted to ride him for at least the first few saddlings but he knew from that colt's action that slipping a saddle on his back wouldn't scare nor faze him no more than when the horse blanket had been strapped on him in the box car and when trailed into the ranch from the railraod, and a rider slipping up in the saddle afterwards, especially Virginia, wouldn't spook him any nor make him want to act up. He wasn't built that way, and wether Virginia would be on his back or on the ground beside him would be all the same to his nature.

Another thing was, Virginia was a mighty fair hand with range bred horses and her string couldn't be classed as what goes for ladies' saddle stock. She'd broke quite a few of them herself and even tho she didn't profess to be a bronco buster she could hold her own with some mighty spooky ones. She had no fear nor thought but what she could easy handle Colonel no matter what he might get in his head to do.

But she went easy with him, took much more time and pains than any of the range bred colts she'd broke. She at first gave him a good brushing and sort of slicked him all up, then she slipped her saddle on him, in as easy a way as tho he'd been saddled many times before, and he didn't even bat an eye. It was a very different and some heavier saddle than his breed ever gets to see but it felt and sat well on his back and he didn't seem to mind it there none at all. He just sniffed at the stirrups hanging down on each side of him then nosed the girl, as much as to say "Well, what now?"

The bridle came next, over the hackamore that was already on his head, it was of a light headstall and snaffle bit. The bit was the only thing that bothered him so far and he tried to work it out with his tongue but of course with no luck, and being it didn't hurt he'd soon enough get used to it.

That all done she tied up the hackamore rope and bridle reins to the saddle horn, giving him plenty of freedom and still tight enough so as not to slip a foot into 'em in case he put his head down. Then he was left loose in the big corral to figure and get used to the rigging and bridle by himself.

Colonel made a pretty picture going around the corral with the outfit on him, but Charro was more in wondering at his long legged pardner packing such a rig, without making a fuss and as tho he'd done it all his life. With him he'd been sort of scared of such a contraption a setting on it, bucking it off or get out from under it in some way or other. He didn't follow Colonel around the corral then, and if he started to come near he'd get out of his way.

Virginia left Colonel be until he got used to the bit some and to packing the saddle, then when he stopped, like as if there'd been enough of the first lesson, she walked to him, unloosened the rope and reins, led him into the stable and unsaddled him. Then she gave him a handful of crushed grain and turned him loose to roll and think over that first lesson. Charro was handed a handful of grain too and then the two was turned out in the pasture again.

The proceedings was about the same on the next day, only not so long with just packing saddle and bridle, for then Virginia also eased herself into the saddle, and now Colonel was some more interested, but not at all flustered at the girl a sitting up there in the middle of him and her hundred and ten pounds didn't faze him no more than the thirty-five pound saddle bad. He stood still for a few seconds, like just wondering what to do, and then she pulled on one bridle rein, turning his head, and with a light slap of the end of the reins on the opposite side he moved the direction his head had been turned. She then turned him on the other side, both sides that way a few times, then straight ahead or just around the corral.

In half an hour of working him easy that way she had him go, turn and stop whichever way she wanted him without much trouble. Then she got off him and let him stand for a spell, and when she got on him again she now broke him into a trot to in time turn him one side then the other without slowing him down on the gait.

Stopping and making him go as she wanted would take the longest to have him do really well, but the colt was cool headed and that would come in good time. After trotting him around the corral some, turning him, stopping him, getting off and on him time and again and his behaving so well all the way thru, Virginia was very satisfied with that second day's workout. She was pleased with the way he seemed so willing and anxious to learn whatever she wanted to teach him, and with his being that way it wouldn't of went well to try to teach him too many things at once. That would be apt to confuse and excite him so as to fretting then he wouldn't be learning any more.

Too long a times at first saddlings are no good either, for when getting tired, the colt will lose interest and

is apt to go to sulking, and maybe try some tricks, then
he wont learn nothing to the good.

Virginia didn't work on Colonel for much more than
an hour that second day, and after another good brushing which he liked, along with another handful of grain,
and no more, he was turned out in the pasture with
Charro again. Charro didn't like such mysterious goings
on, for he sort of feared he might be next most any time
and that wouldn't go well with him.

But he didn't need have no fear because colts are
not broken to ride or work on the range before they're
three year olds, and most of the time at four or five,
and on up. So, Charro not being of the race horse type
still had some years to go before saddle leather would
touch him. Maybe many if he ever got away again.

Colonel, not having showed any signs of bull-headed-
ness or foolishness at the first two saddlings, was rode
outside of the corral for the third one, a time when
most range broncs are apt to bust loose at something
or other on account of the feeling of more freedom in
the open and to do as they felt inclined.

But it was all the same with Colonel and he was as
easy to handle outside of the corral as in, even easier,
for there was more room, less stopping and turning,
and more interesting with Virginia on his back and
sometimes talking to him. With the openness of the
country ahead and all around him he felt of near the
same freedom as he had when drifting along with
Charro, only now, somehow more at ease and secure with
the close company of the human, like part of him.

That ride was only a short one and was so enjoyed by both the girl and the horse that there was none of it being done inside the corral no more. The colt's training went on outside from then on and for two or three hours every day or so.

And the riding wasn't all plain poking or trotting along roads, for there was always cattle not so far from the ranch, some that as before would need Virginia's checking up on most every day, and winding around in looking thru the bunches, sometimes having to hit on a high lope so's to get a close look at some wilder one would all be variety that went well with the high geared colt. He liked them cattle that would give him a little run. But it was hard for him to get it into his head to stop and turn when a fast running critter was passed, and there, Virginia was careful in stopping and turning him so he wouldn't get to fighting his head (jerking it sideways and up and down). She handled him with the hackamore then most of the time, using the bit very little.

She wanted the colt to dodge with or against the critter, pass and turn 'er if need be or whatever was wanted done with the horned one, as her good cowhorses would do. It had taken her plenty of time and hard work amongst stock to teach them good cowhorses of hers what all they knew. But they'd been of that breed, get to taking as much interest in handling cattle as their rider did.

Colonel was plenty intelligent, very willing, and cool headed enough, and even tho Virginia had got him some interested with cow work and he would perk an ear at the ornery critter he didn't develop much heart in the handling of 'em. It didn't seem to be in him, didn't have the knack, and after a couple of months of handling of 'em, a couple of hours or so most every day he hadn't took to or learned as much as her cowhorses had in their first week of breaking.

He was about the same way with neckreining, where the horse is teached to turn by the touch of the rein on the side of his neck, a touch and pull of the rein on the left side turns him to the right, and the same on the right side turns him to the left. All fast turning horses like the cowhorse and polo pony are trained to that, and at all riding where the rider uses only one hand on the reins. Like with the cowboy he has to have a free hand, especially while roping, one to hold the coils along with the reins and the other to throw the loop, also with the polo player he has to have one free arm and hand to use his mallet.

Colonel was a little limbernecked at neckreining, that is he'd learned to turn his head and neck the direction he was wanted to plenty easy but his body wouldn't turn with it so well nor so quick. He done much better when both hands was used on the reins, like with a buggy horse, academy or race horse, for that seemed to steady him more especially in a lope or run. Virginia handled him that way at the first couple of saddlings, like with all colts when first started, then she of course started to neckreining him, more and more while handling cattle, where a colt learns that the quickest. But he didn't answer to that very well even then. She tried both hackamore and snaffle reins but neither seemed to work any better, and even tho he done fair enough for the time he'd been rode she didn't think he'd ever be what's called a well reined horse.

But maybe he'd come to it, she hoped, maybe just take more time. There was one good thing sure tho, and that's how quick he could catch up to a bunch-quitter without even *trying* to run, and what a calf roping horse he'd make for rodeos, if he could be teached to stop and keep the rope tight after the calf was caught and the rider had slid off the saddle to tie it down.

Virginia had shook a loop off of him a few times and Colonel showed only very little interest, no fear, and that had no meaning to him. Then one day, while her dad was riding along with her, some interested in Colonel's progress, and coming to a good sized fall calf in one of the herds, he told her to dab her rope on that one and see how the colt would act.

"All right," Virginia laughed, shaking out a loop, "but you'll have to 'heel it' (roping the calf by the hind feet) because I dont believe I can 'bust' the calf to lay. Colonel cant be handled well enough for that as yet."

The big strong calf lit into a run soon as he seen he was singled out, and Colonel, sensing that with the loop in Virginia's hand there'd be some new game to play and the calf would have some part in it, lit after him as she wanted to, like a streak— So much like a streak that the calf was caught up to and passed before she could make a fair aim with her loop. The calf then dodged back behind the horse and was safe in the middle of the herd again by the time she got Colonel stopped and turned.

Cal shook his head and laughed. "Good thing you didn't catch that calf," he says, "because if you had at the speed you went by him you might of jerked his head plum off his shoulders.

"But let's try it again," and so saying he rode into the herd, manouvered thru it until his chance come and then spurted onto the calf to cut him out in good speed again.

Virginia, outside of the herd and with loop ready, set Colonel after the calf once more, at the same speed, and even tho the calf had a good start and going mighty fast, as such calves can, he was caught up to within the same distance as the head start he'd had. In other words, Colonel had been twice as fast, and that's going some, as any cowboy will vouch.

And this time, Virginia had been prepared, her loop speeded to reach over the calf's head and draw up around the neck just before Colonel passed him, and now was the question to hold and keep the colt from passing. But no chance, too much speed and which only the horse himself can check up on at the right time, when trained to roping. Colonel wasn't, and at the speed he was going there was no checking him up, not until he hit the end of the rope, and then the heavy calf at the other end done the checking up, near jerking Colonel over backwards.

Colonel hadn't of course expected any such a jerk,

maybe he would the next time. But anyhow that slowed him down sudden and so that as he got his balance again, Virginia turned him and made him face the tight rope and the husky calf, now flat on his side, at the other end. That calf had took quite some tumble but had only the wind knocked out of him as he landed so hard. (It's mighty near impossible to hurt one of them six or eight month old range calves, raised by their mothers' side and milk (no skimmed milk) and all the hay and grass they can eat. A jump off a thirty foot bank would hardly faze 'em.)

Knowing that Colonel hadn't as yet got wise to a rope and hold it tight, Cal had rode onto the calf at near the same time Virginia had turned her horse, and soon as the rope slackened he was off his saddle and took the rope off before that young one got his wind and could get up. And not any too soon, for the calf scrambled up as the rope grazed off his nose, and now, being on the peck (fight) he butted the laughing Cal back up on his horse before he went back for the herd.

"Thought you said you couldn't bust that calf to lay." Cal laughed on as he rode up to the side of Virginia again.

"Well," she laughed back. "It wasn't my fault, and it's a wonder Colonel didn't get jerked down too."

"A good yearling would of done it," says Cal, "and a grown steer would of broke him in two. But a few more jerks like that with that calf, for a starter, will make him pay attention and that's plenty heavy enough for him. . . . If he could be made to stop soon as the calf

Then the heavy calf at the other end done the checking up,
near jerking Colonel over backwards

is caught he'd sure be a top one, with that speed of his.
But I guess it aint in him to stop at such a time, because
I see he can't stand to have anything be ahead of him,
not when there's any running to be done."

"Maybe Brad could break him of that, teach him

when and how to stop. Maybe one summer of rodeo calf roping would do it."

Cal looked at his daughter in surprise. "Would you let Brad have him that way?" he asked.

"Well," she shrugged, "maybe I would. I can't help but always feel that he's as much his as mine, and if he'd be of good use to him that way, why——"

"Huh, huh," Cal grunted, "—but he'd have to be trained a considerable out here before he'd be much good in a rodeo arena. And even then, I doubt if he'd take to it, that's not in his line of breeding."

Such an idea or thought was of course mostly only talk, and then, like out of the clear sky, there come something else to Cal's mind.

"You know, Virginia," he says, "I got to thinking. I got to thinking that this colt you're riding is a very valuable horse, valuable for his speed, more so to others that way than he might ever be to you—and what if he should ever get away again?

"What do you mean, dad?" she asked, puzzled.

"Just this. He ought to be branded."

Virginia thought on that for a spell, then she said, "But I don't see where it's necessary for *him* to be branded, not on this range and where everybody knows of him. Besides if anybody else got him we could always identify him and prove he's ours."

"Why, Virginia," Cal says, grinning at her. "I'm surprised at you talking that way when you know better and doggone well that it don't matter what kind of a horse he might be the brand is the only thing that really identifies him. It's registered, and before six months old every colt or calf should bear the brand of their owners on their hide, or they might come up missing with some others' brand on 'em, wether they was on this range or not, and nothing can be done about it unless it can be proved that the colt or calf was by their mothers' side and taken away from them before being branded. That's impossible to prove after a couple of weeks' time. With this colt wether he's found on or off this range he'd be some great temptation for any rider who'd happen to see him, and then, supposing he got out where mustang runners got a hold of him. They wouldn't know who he belonged to and he'd be shipped out of the country with other mustangs. You could of course claim him if you was there and you had a couple of witnesses to prove he's yours, but you would never know he was caught or shipped nor where he'd went to.

"But with your brand on him that makes it all very different, it would then be plain horse stealing against anybody trying to run off with him. With the registered brand, in state and inspectors' books, he can be traced and identified anywheres. Another thing is, if he gets away and he gets caught, all the finder would have to do is look up the brand book and the brand of the horse there would give the name and address of his owner.

"No matter how good a description might be given of an animal as to color, age, size or markings that dont get anywheres nor is paid attention to once far enough away. The brand is what counts and makes any man more than hesitate to move on with him, unless that man is a horse thief, and then he's taking big chances and liable to suffer plenty of consequences.

"Like an old cow thief I once knew often used to say, "I'll take to beef cattle every time, but no horses for me, because cattle soon go to the slaughter house and that's the end of 'em, but with a horse he'll live a long time and always advertising the brand that might sooner or later give you away."

"Of course some brands can be changed but the changer has to be quite an artist to do that so well as to get by a good stock inspector——"

Virginia finally had to interrupt. "I know all of that fairly well, dad," she said. "And I still dont see where it's necessary that Colonel should be branded. His kind is not supposed to be. Besides I wont ever want to turn him out on the range. And now that the blacksmith has put that fool-proof latch, as he calls it, on the new pole gates of the pasture I don't see how he can ever get away again."

Cal only shrugged and grinned a little. "All right," he says, "but if he was mine there'd be my brand on him before sundown come this evening. His kind may not be supposed to be branded, but I used to have many of his kind and, by japers, every one of them I kept on the ranch here sure was branded. It sure didn't interfere with their good speed either, made me feel like they was sure enough mine, while I owned 'em, and also proud of them packing my iron because the most of 'em I raised here turned out to be winners.

"Of course it's very different in some states, where

there's no brand laws and a brand is looked at only
as a blemish. And true enough, it'd be only unnecessary
and foolish to brand a horse there. Because, in such
states, the horses dont run free and mix with others
as ours do on the range here, where they can go as they
please for a hundred miles or more in some places. So,
being all horses should be branded in this territory any
unbranded one that gets away is apt to be anybody's
for the taking, anybody who puts his brand on him
first.

"That aint a good feeling to have about a horse of
your own, just on account he aint branded. Especially
when you think a lot of him—. No sirree, and if I was
you, Virginia, I'd sure slap my iron on this colt of yours
right quick. I'd feel better about it, if I was you."

Virginia couldn't help but smile some at the concern
her dad was showing over the colt. "You seem to 've
taken quite a sudden interest in Colonel," she says.
"May I ask what caused that?"

"I don't give a hoot so much about the colt," he came
back at the girl, sort of quick. "It's you I'm thinking
of, the way you fretted, moped and carried on the
time he got away, and if that was ever to happen again
you might not be so lucky in getting him back. You'd
have many more chances at that if you had your brand
on him, and I know that for your sake I wouldn't be
near so fretful myself then.

"I'll tell you what, Virginia, queer I didn't think of
it before, but you could use your mother's iron. It's
a mighty neat little horse brand, goes on the left

shoulder, and has been by her on as good as there could be in horseflesh. It's easy to read and couldn't be changed so the original wouldn't show. We called it the Comet, just a star with tails, like this," he traced it on the palm of his hand as he rode— "By the way, there was a breed of horses and there's still trace of their blood can be found now and again. Your mother would be mighty pleased of you using her brand, and it would please me too."

The two had been on their way back to the ranch as that talk had been going on, and after a lull in the conversation, Virginia turned to her dad, saying,

"I guess you win again, as usual, Dad— But what about Charro, are we going to brand him too?"

"Why, yes, I think we just as well while we're at it. But if you have no objections I think I'll put one of my own horse irons on him. It would be better known than your mother's which we'll put on Colonel."

Virginia had no objections as to what iron was put on Charro, and, as she said, he wasn't her's but Brad's or her dad's mostly— So that's how come that being the branding was now decided on that same evening would be as good a time as any to do and have it over with.

On their return to the ranch, while Virginia rode into the pasture to get Charro, Cal got busy building a branding fire in one corner of the corral, then digging up his wife's branding iron which had been carefully put away and hadn't been used for over twenty years he layed it on the fire to once more be heated. One of

his own old ones ⊂ was layed alongside of it for
Charro it was the ℃, for Cal Goodwin.

The branding of a gentle horse, one that can be led
to stand without fighting, is a simple operation and
doesn't last long. The gentle horse is just held, doesn't
have to be thrown or even hobbled and by the man holding him putting a hand over one eye on the side he's
to be branded, or blindfold, few horses will seldom move
a hoof or more than flinch as the hot iron is placed on
their hide by the other man. It's only for a few seconds,
and after it's done the horse might only do a little
twitching at the seared part then go right back to
grazing soon as he's turned free again. None at all the
worse for the experience and seeming to hold no fear
nor grudge against the human for it. . . . But of course,
after all, a brand is a burn and, as Cal had said, would
be very foolish and unnecessary to do in some countries.
But on the western ranges, where stockmen run up to
many thousand head of stock it's very necessary to
brand, even to the gentlest close to the ranch. No stockman has any time to do anything that's unnecessary,
much less cause pain to any of his stock, even if only
for a few seconds, such as branding, if it wasn't abso-
lutely necessary.

Virginia held the horses while Cal done the branding,
neither Colonel nor Charro made any fuss as the red
hot iron seemed to only touch their hide, after that was
over some heavy healing salve of Cals own mixture that
would also keep flies away was spread thick on the fresh
made brands and the two was left to go to the pasture,

marked for life and protected from any rider who before would of figured the colts as easy pickings and
very much worth getting, especially the tall dark one.

So now, no matter where these two would graze or
range the well known brands they was packing would
be recognized and respected, they wasn't nobody's
horses no more, and Virginia did feel some better about
that brand of ownership on Colonel's shiny left shoulder. Her mother's brand and now proud it was her very
own.

SOMEBODY'S HORSE NOW

CHAPTER ELEVEN

CHARRO LEADS AGAIN

THE branding of the colts had been done just in good time, or, as Virginia wondered was it only a test as to how good the brands would hold when, one fine morning, a week or so after the branding, and going into the pasture to get her saddle horses she couldn't see hide nor hair of either Colonel or Charro. Then looking down the pasture and seeing one of the new pole gates with the "fool proof" latches opened she didn't have to guess twice as to what had happened. Them two colts, with Charro leading, had hit out again.

But as she got the remaining saddle horses in the corral and caught the one she wanted she found there was one of the missing. This one was an old gray pensioner that hadn't been rode for years and had been brought in to be doctored for distemper. He'd been turned in the pasture with the few saddle horses to recuperate on the green feed for a few days before he'd be turned out again.

That old gray had been the only one missing along with the colts, and knowing as Virginia did where he ranged she had high hopes as she started out after the runaways that she'd soon catch up with 'em. For one thing, they didn't have more than one night's start, and figuring the colts would sure be with the gray it would be just a nice day's ride getting 'em.

So sure was she of finding the colts with the gray that she didn't look for their tracks after going thru the last ranch gate but rode straight on and at a good clip for the gray's range. Virginia knew that range well, every horse on it and where each one or bunch run, and it didn't surpise her any when along near noon she seen the gray about a mile ahead of her, just grazing along slow and towards his range which was still some distance further on.

It didn't bother her none that she didn't see the two darker ones, Colonel and Charro, for, being that country was very hilly, them two could be somewhere close by the gray, in some ravine or where she couldn't see them until she rode nearer.

But she was due for disappointment, for as she rode nearer the gray she soon seen he was very much alone. The gray sort of sprinted around at the sight of her, more like a three year old wild one than the thirty year old pensioned cowhorse he was, throwed up his head and tail, snorted and whistled loud and then hit out cross-country like as if all damnation was after him, for his range and at a speed that would of bothered Virginia's good horse to follow.

Virginia just watched the old gray go, and her hopes at seeing the colts faded right then. For if they'd been anywheres close to the gray they'd sure come out of wherever they was at, acted wild too, and followed him. They'd at least showed up to see what all he was running about.

Now, as she sat her horse, watching the running gray in the distance, she knew then that the colts hadn't followed him very far out from the ranch. There was now only one thing for her to do and that was turn back and "cut" for their tracks, above where she figured they'd most likely left the gray.

But there again, as she rode, it came to her of the fall before, how they'd both been found away on the other side of the ranch and not at all like from the badlands, which was far on this side of it. As it was they might be working around the ranch to get on the other side. But if so she'd be bound to come acrost their tracks anyway, where they left off from the gray's.

She was riding slow watching for them tracks now, and she was pleased when she finally come acrost 'em. But they wasn't heading like to circle around the ranch and get on the other side of it as she'd expected, instead they was going for the horse range and towards the badlands beyond.

It was now middle afternoon but Virginia rode on along the familiar tracks for quite a ways, until she come to a deep water hole, and there, with so many fresh tracks of other horses that'd come to water, she lost the ones of the colts. But she had the general direction of where they was headed, and would of circled on further to find the tracks again, but it was getting late, there was a long twenty mile ride back to the ranch and she turned back. She'd be on their trail again early the next morning.

It was away after dark when she got back to the ranch. Her dad and Anne had waited up for her, and while Virginia was easing her appetite, her dad told her how he'd figured the gates to be opened and the colts getting out. Virginia had been doing plenty of wondering about that herself.

"That old renegade gray, old White Cloud, is the one to blame for them gates being opened." Cal grinned. "I looked good for shoe or boot tracks around 'em after you left and there wasn't any but yours, but there was plenty of old White Cloud's. I can tell his old pigeon-toed tracks easy, and I could see that he done a lot of stomping around the gate in studying of ways to work the "fool-proof" patent so's to open it.

"Old White Cloud is no fool, and as I got to thinking and remembering, that old wise one used to sort of take pride in opening gates with all sorts of different fixings on 'em and letting the stock out, even if sometimes he didn't care to go himself. There was only one kind of fixing on a gate I figure he couldn't open, and that was when it was chained and locked. I wouldn't of been too surprised if he'd worked even that. . . . Yep, after investigating all around, asking all the help on the ranch and everything I'm sure that old White Cloud is the culprit. The ranch blacksmith here who invented that riggin' thinks I'm crazy but when I get that old white devil in again sometime I'll prove it to him he's the one who can sure work that fool proof gate patent of his."

Virginia couldn't help but laugh a little with her dad at his telling of old White Cloud's wisdom in opening gates.

"Yes," she said, "but if he's the guilty one dont you

ever have him in the same pasture with Colonel and Charro again, or any other horse we want to keep close to home."

"I sure won't," Cal said, still chuckling some. "But I never thought, or I mean, I'd forgot about that old calawag's tricks. You see, it's been about ten years since I stopped riding him, and a feller can forget quite a few things in that time, but not with that wise old wolloper—I dont know how he learned such freaky tricks. He never was no pet. If he was I wouldn't think so much of it, but he was born and raised in the hills, was a tough one to break and you could hardly lead him into a barn even during the worst of weather, and right today I'll bet he'd still do a good job of bucking. No, sir. I cant figure out that gate opening streak of his."

But now, there was the getting of the colts back again, and that wouldn't be easy. They now had twenty-four hours' start, would be travelling right along and take only short spells to graze now and again, and that way they'd be many more hours in the lead before they could be caught up to, to wherever they was headed, and that's where would be the puzzle, where they'd be headed.

It was early light the next morning when Virginia rode out for the horse range, where she'd lost trail of the colts the day before. There was of course more fresh horse tracks by then, tracks of all sizes, from few-day-old colts to the size of full grown horses, and it would be near impossible to trail Colonel and Charro on thru them. But knowing from the day before the general direction they'd taken she looked thru only a few bunches of the range horses that was closest, then after going thru the horse range she made a sort of half circle, cutting for their tracks, and to her pleasure she found 'em again. But also to her surprise them tracks led straight on for the badlands and not at all circling around the ranch to where the colts had been found the fall before, where she'd believed was Charro's range. And now, with the badlands to ride into, or cross, to wherever they might be headed for, that would be a man-sized job, a good man who knew that country and mounted on a mighty good horse. Virginia took pride in being all woman. She respected and never tried to do whatever was really a man's job, and she knew that hitting them badlands was a sure enough man's job, not any man's, but one who knew what he was about and what to do when he got in them, and found the colts.

Brad would be the man but he was away again, with the bucking stock and following the rodeos. The contracts for the stock, and with his contesting would keep him away until late in the fall. There was one good old cowboy at one of the camps who might do but her dad had plenty of use for him. The other two cowboys was good men too but mostly with regular cow work, and there's quite some difference between that and wild horse running. And wild horse running it would be because, as Virginia figured, the colts would soon get with the wild ones and then be as hard to catch. She would talk that over with her dad.

There was one good old cowboy at one of the camps who might do

Before turning her horse back for the ranch that day, Virginia, wanting to make sure of the colts' rambling, followed their trail plum up to the badlands and quite a ways into 'em. She could see that their tracks was over a day old, also was sure they'd kept going right on. To catch up with 'em she'd have to stay in the badlands that night and hit on their trail again at the light of dawn. Even then she knew she'd lost their trail in stony or wind blown places, and if she did catch up with 'em they'd most likely be with some wild bunch by then and if so she knew there'd be no more catching Colonel, much less Charro, unless she got 'em cornered alone or in a trap.

Then again there was her horse, a very good horse, but she'd come a long roundabout way that day and he was now ganted up and tired, also thirsty. Grass was in mighty scattering patches everywheres around and there was no water. She'd have to hobble him and take big chances of losing him. The thought of being left afoot in that country didn't strike her as at all pleasant. Besides she was some hungry herself, not having et since daybreak that morning, thirsty too, and she knew better than drink water from them badlands if she did find some. So, all in all, it more and more struck her as a full-sized man's job, a hardened mustang runner's, to go on in that country and catch up with the colts.

But she'd only wanted to make sure as to which way the colts had gone and if they'd keep a going, and now that she was satisfied as to that she turned her horse back for the ranch and in as straight a course as her horse would take. It was plenty steep at times.

A light was still a burning in the main room of the
house when she got there that night, and her dad and
Anne was still sort of up and waiting for her. That is,
they hadn't lost much sleep at doing that. Her dad,
his boots and all but his hat still on, was stretched out
on the davenport, while Anne had made herself just as
comfortable in his pet overstuffed chair, the kind with
a foot rest that springs out from underneath and a back
that can be adjusted to any incline. Both had been
asleep until Virginia opened the door and walked in.

Her dad was the first to set up and blink at her. Then
rubbing his eyes, he grinned. "Well. Good morning,
daughter."

Anne didn't say anything but just sort of jumped
up, smiled at her and hit for the kitchen, and paying
no attention to Virginia asking her not to bother, that
she didn't want anything, she went right on rattling
the stove lids and stirring up a fire, remarking the while
that she'd have the coffee and things all hot and ready
for her in a jiffy.

"Well, if that's the case," Cal says, now full awake,
"I think I'll have my coffee and little breakfast now,
being you're at it. It'll soon be daybreak and I've sure
had all the sleep I wanted. But," he added on, looking
at the girl, "better take care of Virginia first, she must
be powerful tired and hungry."

Virginia sat in the chair Anne had just left and
smiled. "I am tired," she smiled on, "I think I'll be
able to sleep too."

"I should think so," Anne chips in from the kitchen door. "Come, pull your boots off, bathe your face a little and by that time I'll have everything on the table for you. You'll rest better after you eat a little something."

Cal stood up, stretched and walked outside, took a few lungsful of the early morning air, sat down on the edge of the big porch and rolled a smoke. "Doggone that ridge running Colonel," he says, after the first puff. "I'll bet he's going to be hard to get this time, and Brad and Red gone too." He thought on for a while. He didn't want Virginia to worry and ride herself and her horses ragged for that colt as she had the year before. She'd sure do it again too—and here he of a sudden thought of a way of relieving her of that, of somebody who'd sure get him and quick. That is, quick as any other could.

He went back in the house, all smiles and remarking that this early morning air sure made a feller feel good. "Better than all night air, aint it?" he says, grinning at Virginia, who by then had got into a house dress and felt some refreshed.

Anne soon brought in a pot of steaming coffee, followed by a regular hot breakfast and the three sat down to it, the talk was up in the air for a spell, until after a second cup of coffee, and then Virginia spoke up, of her long ride. She didn't have to tell of her failure in finding the colts, but as she said, she did know for sure where they'd went before she turned back, and that was away into the badlands.

That was aplenty to satisfy Cal. He didn't ask no questions and gave her no advice as to what she should of done, instead he only remarked that she'd made a powerful big ride for a little girl like her, or even for a big man, and that she'd done fine in finding their tracks again and knowing for sure which country they went into.

"That will help a considerable," he said, as he got up from the table. "And listen, young lady," he went on, pointing a finger at her. "I want you to stay home today and rest up. I'll relieve you of hunting for them colts, and if the way I do dont suit you why you can take up the trail where I left off. Now catch yourself a nap and let your saddle rest."

With that last, and light pat on her cheek, he picked up his jacket and out the door he went, saying. "I'll be back tonight."

The two women looked at one another, wondering, as Cal went out the door. It was still hardly daybreak, and they wondered some more when a few minutes later they heard the purr of his big car and then, looking out the window, seen the headlights of it headed for the main road a mile away, the main one leading to town. It was all very mysterious.

Anne turned to Virginia. "Why," she says in surprise. "Looks like he's going to town— That's not the direction the colts would be, and besides how would he catch 'em in a car?"

Virginia only smiled. "He's not going after the colts, Anne," she said, "not right now anyway. But you can be sure he's got some good scheme of getting 'em. We might find out what it is when he gets back, and right now I'm going to catch up on some sleep and rest, as he and you said for me to do."

The womenfolk would of wondered plenty more if along before noon that same day they'd seen Cal drive into the County Seat, straight up to the Court House and into that building, then again when he planked down two thousand dollars in cash for bail money to release one bewiskered but smiling small man from behind the bars of the cell block there.

Them womenfolk would of thought it mighty mysterious then too. For this small man, of around thirty, was none other than the well known horsethief and mustang runner, Blackie Cooper. He'd been arrested by stock inspectors a few weeks before for mixing and trying to ship branded horses not belonging to him along with some mustangs he'd caught. He'd of course worked the brands over, but not quite well enough to get by the wise eyes of one of the inspectors who one time had been quite an artist at that himself. Besides, there was one especial horse that was a dead give away, regardless of the well changed brand on him, for an inspector knew that horse well, also the man who owned him.

Anyway, Blackie would be locked up, he wouldn't plead guilty. So the stiff bail was set, and now the trial would not be before that fall. He'd had to pace his cell for the long months up to that time, because neither him nor his two pardners, who was still out in the hills with the saddle horses, could of put up nowheres near such an amount as two thousand dollars to get him out on bail. He had no other friends he could call on-to for any such an amount. Then Cal, having heard of his predicament, came along.

It struck Blackie queer he'd never thought of Cal. He'd rode for him for quite a while some years before, when Cal still had some of his racing stock, and the both had thought a lot of one another. He'd rode longer for Cal, but when Cal finally lost all his racing stock, with only a few saddle horses left, and having to go back to riding after cattle, why Blackie had quit. Cattle was too slow for him no matter how wild they might be. He was used to horses, he'd liked to train them racing colts of Cal's, and even tho raised on and used to range horses he was a good hand with them thoroughbreds. Cal came near taking him along as a jockey a couple of times, but there'd been always some new colts for him to take care of. Blackie would of been a mighty good jockey too, for, along with knowing as much as he did about horses he also had the good jockey weight. Light and wiry.

When Cal lost his horses, Blackie lost heart and went back to running wild ones, what he'd been raised at doing. He run and caught many wild horses in different western states and worked for horse outfits in between times, but never for cow outfits, and there was one man Blackie rode for and never stole a horse from. That man was Cal, and Cal knew and appreciated that. Now he was showing his appreciation.

Blackie lost heart and went back to running wild ones, what he'd been raised at doing

Not only that, which maybe didn't call for appreciation, but Cal needed him. There was no better mustang
runner in that country, and he needed him to get that
Colonel colt back for Virginia. Cal knew that with
Charro's lead, hitting for the badlands, them two was
headed for the wild horse country which was beyond.
He knew that they'd soon join some wild bunch there
and that then, Colonel would be as hard or maybe
harder to get near than any of the wild ones, and
Blackie, he figured, was about the only man who could
manouver to catch him. If Colonel was with a bunch of
wild ones he'd have to catch that bunch in order to get
him. If not he'd be with Charro, and that little grulla
would have to be caught too, which would be just as
hard to do if not harder than catching a whole bunch.

As far as trusting Blackie to deliver Colonel when
caught and not to quit the country, leaving Cal loser
on the bail money, Cal hardly gave any thought of that.
He knew Blackie enough and felt he could well depend
on him, more now than ever before.

There was no talk about that as the two et a noon
meal at a restaurant. The main talk was of Colonel and
getting him. As the talk went on that way, the lay of
the country where Colonel might be in, Cal learned that
Blackie had been running horses in that same country
only the year before, and not only that, but, to Cal's
surprise, he gave him the description of Colonel and
Charro. For Blackie was the same mustang runner who
that year before had caught the four young studs of
the bunch Colonel and Charro had took up with, them

and the two old renegades. He was the one who'd marvelled at Colonel's speed as the two broke away and he rode on with the four studs, figuring on getting Colonel and Charro on the next day.

Well, that made it all easy. He knew the country and the horses he was to get. It would be all easy but maybe the catching, and Blackie didn't seem to be worried about that. He still had his saddle horses and outfit with his pardners. He'd have his two pardners move camp back near that country of Charro's home range, and now all he wanted was a saddle and a good horse till he got to his own, somebody to show him the trail where at Colonel and Charro went into the badlands and he'd do the rest from there on.

"Gadamighty, Mr. Goodwin." Blackie busted out as him and Cal was driving back to the ranch. "This is one time when I'm going to be powerful happy to doing something else along with running mustangs."

"What something else?" asks Cal, having a sort of a hunch.

"Nell's bells, Cal. You know what I mean."

CHAPTER TWELVE

WINNER TAKES ALL

IT had been a month since Colonel and Charro had got out of the pasture and away, and then one day a rider came to the Hip-O ranch leading a saddled horse. It was the horse that Cal had loaned Blackie some three weeks before, pretty well rode down but not hurt in any way, only needing a rest. And the rider was Blackie, looking like he also needed a rest.

Him and Cal got together by the corrals that evening. "Well, I seen him," he grinned. "Yep, I seen him quite a few times, but just streaks of him. Why, man, it'd take the combined speed of two of the fastest horses in this country to get close enough for a good look at brown colt.

"But I'm sure it was him I seen, I mean the one you call Colonel, and how that colt can and likes to run. The reason I'm sure is because he's still with the little grulla, and that little feller is sure no slouch either, but he's like tied and standing still when that brown unlimbers them long legs of his. He'll run big circles around him while the little feller levels out to his best towards wherever he wants to go. But that little feller is the brains of the two when it comes to dodging every way of catching him, and his pardner sure knows it. That little feller has spotted every blind and water trap

235

there is in the country. He'll never go near one, and as far as to corner him against rims or box canyons so's to get a chance to rope him why it'd be foolish to even think of it. Another thing is he's never in same part of the country or runs the same direction twice. On that account we cant build a trap for him because we wouldn't know if he'd ever run the direction of it, alone get him into it.

"We all three went after him time and again, used every scheme we knew of to get him one way or another but the wise little devil seemed to see thru 'em all and get by everytime, the tall one just having a lot of fun with us by making distance the way the little one pointed.

"We even tried to relay on 'em, the three of us stationed some ten miles apart, but they'd get away even halfways before they could be got to the second relay rider. Then, we got to thinking we could easy enough trap the tall one if we somehow could get rid of the wise little leader. There'd been only one way of doing that, and that'd been to shoot him. But none of us wanted to do that. We later seen that it wouldn't of been of any use anyway because there come times when the tall one himself would take turn and be the proud leader of some bunch, one bunch one time and another bunch the next, and even tho the little feller would always be in the same bunches with him, that went to show that even without his little pardner the tall one would only fanned his tail at us and soon join up with one of them bunches.

"He might of course been easier caught then, if he got with some bunch with not so wise a leader as Charro, but it seems like that Colonel colt now has took on a lot of little Charro's wisdom and turning out to be quite some leader himself. He's not the ignorant colt he was last year. He didn't know which way to run then, but now he acts like it's a lot of fun to outrun and outwit a rider. With Charro it's all seriousness, near like a matter of life and death in making his getaways, but with Colonel he just sort of plays with us, and when we get a chance to pocket or crowd him towards a trap he's up and gone in a puff of dust." Blackie snapped his fingers. "Just like that."

"Huh! Some horse," grunted Cal. "Sure worth getting— But how do you aim to proceed to do that now, Blackie?" He asked.

"The same as I been doing. That's all can be done, and trust to luck for a good chance at that. It would be mostly by pure good luck, and lots of it. A feller never can tell when such a chance might come, but I thought I'd better come over and let you know in case you'd be wondering, and bring your horse and saddle back. I had to use him some, and he's a little legweary."

"That's all right," says Cal, "when there's work to be done." Then he asked, "How're you doing with the other wild ones, catching many?"

"Pretty good," says Blackie, "and along with staying on Colonel and Charro's trail mostly and trying to get them we've caught near enough now to make up two carloads."

"No more branded ones that you cant answer for, is there?" asks Cal, grinning.

Blackie grinned back a little and just said, "No, not for a while anyway."

"Now," Cal went on, "as to that horse of mine which you brought back, I noticed that your own horse could also use some rest. Better leave him here too and take a couple of mine for a while. I've got plenty here that sure needs riding, good tough circle horses that'll do you fine."

That went more than well with Blackie, and so, the next day Cal went with him to the horse range, drove a bunch into the corrals and from it picked two good fresh ones, leaving the two tired ones in their place.

As Cal had said, they was plenty tough, not only for long rides but also to top off for the start, and little Blackie had to be the rider he was or he'd never got started. For that didn't seem to bother Blackie much, and after that horse's head came up, ready for travel, Cal handed him the lead rope of the other tough horse, opened the corral gate, and bidding the little rider the best of luck, watched him ride on, on towards the badlands and back to the wild horse country.

"Tough and reckless as he's little." Cal remarked as he closed the corral gate on the remaining horses, which he'd later turn out to drift back to the horse range, Blackie's horse with 'em.

Virginia had again got sort of reconciled at Colonel's running away, only she was some disappointed in him this second time. She hadn't blamed him the first time because he didn't know no better then, but this second time, after all the winter's good care, being so gentle and behaving so well under the saddle it was disappointing that he would leave again at the first chance, even tho she knew that Charro had led him on. So, feeling some peeved at the "rascal" she didn't worry so much about him as she had the first time. Then again, she knew where he'd gone and could now take care of himself. There was a good horse hunter steady out to get him, and being she couldn't do no more she took it some easier.

She was of course mighty glad when that horse hunter, Blackie, came with the news that he'd seen him, seen him often, and that some time he might catch and bring him back. For encouragement, Cal had made that seem much more possible than it really was or believed himself. Adding on to that, he sort of painted great stories of the wonders and speed of the colt amongst the wild ones, as a great leader and faster than all of 'em. That was of course supposed to be from Blackie's say so, but he wasn't exaggerating there, and the reason he told her such stories was to at least relieve her of any worries about him.

But it done better than that, she felt proud of him, and with her dad's word paintings she could see him well at the lead of some wild bunch, mane and tail a flying, and—then would come other thoughts, would she ever get him back? Her dad couldn't somehow make any convincing word pictures that him being such a horse could ever be caught.

Cal had been careful not to tell her of the wild horse

cunning the colt had developed. He heard of it off and on as summer wore along, and got to figuring that Colonel was now having too much fun to let himself be caught.

Virginia also heard of such goings on a couple of times that summer. But not from Cal, and as she told him about it one day, he only laughed a little and said sort of encouragingly to her, as well as to himself, "Dont you worry. That running around he's doing is the best thing for him. If all thoroughbreds had such kind of training to develop on they'd be much tougher and still better in every way, footing, endurance, brains and, well, in every way. Colonel is getting just that and a lot of fun to boot, not just mechanical-like, grinding and monotonous work as he'd get in paddocks and tracks like youngsters in schools. His is interesting, where the going is rough and has to use his wits along with his speed.

"Maybe he wont get caught, but I'll bet you a new saddle, you need one anyway, against one of your cheerful smiles that when the snows begin blasting on his rump this fall he'll be drifting in along the fence again as he did last fall."

Virginia had thought of that, and from all she'd heard of his wise ways of dodging loop and traps, she'd come to figure that there was her only hope, when snows would come.

More so when, one day that fall, before the snows did come, Blackie rode in. It wasn't because he'd given up hopes of catching Colonel, but the months he'd been at trying to in every way proved that when as good a mus-

tang runner as he was had failed in that time there wasn't
much use of any others trying.

Virginia knew the reason for Blackie's return and she
admired him for being so true with his word. He'd had
plenty of good horses, his own and belongings to go on
with. But he'd returned in good time for Cal to take him
back to the county seat and to stand trial there in a
case where he'd be most sure to be convicted. Mighty
tough for a man used to so much freedom.

Cal stood by him during the trial. It didn't last long,
and Blackie was sent up for from two to fourteen years.
But the months of freedom that Cal was responsible for
before the trial done much more to turn Blackie against
being careless with others' stock than the prison sen-
tence ever could.

It was a month or so afterwards when, with the rodeo
contracts over with, Brad and Red and Jim returned
with the buckers and longhorns. Then the late fall works
had to be rushed into, and there was no sparing of Brad
and Red to go mustang running and trying to get Colonel
right then, nor for quite a spell. But it was figured it was
just as well, because Colonel couldn't be caught anyway,
and he'd most likely return of his own accord when the
heavy snows come and winter set in, the same as he had
the year before. Virginia was very glad that he was
branded.

But one look at that now alert, wise and confident
long-legged brown colt at the edge of the badlands would
of been plenty to scatter all such hopes of his ever coming back to the ranch of his own accord, regardless of

weather. Now two and a half years old he was far from the same colt of the year before. As to toughness his hide was still thin but he'd got so he could take bumps and stand most any ordinary weather in fair shape. He'd got to handling them long legs of his mighty well too, near as good as Charro in the rough country and to very much more advantage on the halfway level kind.

His so early experiences with lions, wild studs, poison waters and the many dangers of the badlands and wild horse country had left a mighty deep impression in him, especially with him being so young and green at the time, all so strange and out of his line of breeding. With him being that way them experiences had struck him much deeper than it would of with a colt born and raised there and of the wild horse blood. He'd benefited according to that. He hadn't forgot and never would, and with other happenings that followed on now and again with his second year of wild freedom he was more ready and able to compete with 'em.

Thru all of that he wouldn't of had a better teacher and pardner than the natural wise little Charro. He couldn't of lived thru that first summer without him. But then again, if it hadn't been for Charro he'd never ventured into the badlands and the wild horse country, he'd of stayed with the saddle horses in the pasture, and if he had hit out he'd never gone any further than the horse range, if that far. He'd been easy to ride up to and catch anytime, the range horses wouldn't of run much, and so, he wouldn't got that idea into his head to start running and go to outdistancing everything in sight.

So, as it was, little Charro had been the one to lead
him astray, from the well beaten trail to the rough wild
horse country, amongst renegades, and teached him all
the tricks as well as how to take care of himself. But if
Colonel held that against his little pardner or was
ashamed of his actions in any way he anything but
showed it. Instead, he'd got to take pride of being
amongst the wild ones, rolling in the dirt, do all as they
did and how he could beat 'em to leaving a rider in the
distance. He was something like a petted and starched
youngster who'd broke loose from his maid's holt, got
out of her sight and went to mixing with a bunch of rol-
licking rowdies, all strange, some wild and dangerous but
along with a lot of freedom, danger and fun, no low
mischieving or harm doing.

With his teachings and wisdom from the wild ones,
Colonel had got more sure of himself, more bold, for he'd
got to sense danger and know what he'd be getting into
before it was too late, and Charro, now past two years old
too, had also added on more wisdom to his natural wild
instinct. There was no more dodging of strange wild
bunches, and the two together made most grown studs of
such bunches hesitate some before diving into 'em. Some
wouldn't, and when others got too tough, Colonel could
now easy outdistance 'em, Charro would wisely dodge.

All was going fine with Colonel, he was "the king of
all he surveyed" when it come to speed, and he knew it,
and when that fall come, then cold, snow packing winds
hit his rump he didn't no more think of the ranch, the
warm stable and good hay there. That had also got to be

of the past and near as distant as the blue grass meadows where he was born.

And, like in cahoots with him, to make it more easy, that fall didn't come fast and furious as the fall before had. He'd got a chance to grow a better coat of hair, and then the winter that set in was so mild as compared to the one before that it was hardly noticed. There was no steady cold but many warmer spells, and the snow didn't come near so deep. There was times when it would melt so considerable bare ground would show.

Colonel and Charro drifted on to a new and lower range for that winter, where there was more grass and less snow, and in their drifting they'd joined in with a small stud bunch for more company. The stud of that bunch hadn't offered to put up much of a fight. He was a kind of a good natured jughead which is sometimes found amongst all breeds of horses, and it was a wonder how he'd got a hold of his harem of mares and fillies, or how come some other stud hadn't taken 'em away from him. Anyway he had 'em. Colonel and Charro didn't raise no runkus and all went well.

And now, when some other bunch was met and a fighting stud would come out to challenge there'd be three out to meet him, and after sizing up the situation he'd usually only shake his head and turn back to his bunch again.

In all the drifting and country that Colonel and Charro had covered during the summer past and now the winter on they hadn't come acrost either of the two renegade saddle horses they'd run with the fall before, hadn't seen no sign of 'em. Maybe them two wise ones had got weak and poor during the hard winter past and had been caught. Many bunches of wild ones had been caught since that time, for there'd been more mustang runners come to that country than ever before. It could be noticed that the wild ones had thinned down considerable in numbers, and where eight or ten bunches could of been seen in one day's ride the year before there now was only maybe three or four, of the wisest, wildest and fastest ones left.

And one day, during the middle of the winter, the two renegade saddle horses did show up. Charro had been the first one to spot 'em sunning themselves on the side of a tall butte, then the stud spotted 'em, and as he started out to meet 'em, Charro and Colonel followed him.

The palaver with them and the stud was short, no trouble there, and as he started back for his bunch the colts soon renewed their acquaintance with the geldings again, and as they also started back for the bunch the two wise ones sort of tagged along too. It was now a sort of mixed up harem the old stud had, but all got along well, and now, with the added wisdom of the two renegades, it would of took some powerful outside stud to 've come in and tried to take away any of the mares or fillies out of *that* bunch.

That was tried a few times as the bunch drifted and grazed over that range, but with no success, and a couple of the challenging studs hightailed it back to their bunches much faster than they'd come out, glad to be still all together, outside of being short some hide and fur after the meeting was over.

Then one day there come a fiery young stud. He had a nice little bunch of mares, just a few, but he'd fought hard and well to whip out the stud that'd had 'em. That young stud had had quite a few fights afterwards in order to hold his little bunch, and coming out victorious each time he felt pretty cocky and to figuring there wasn't a stud he couldn't whip. And now ambitious to conquer some more and add on to his harem at the same time he kept watch for a likely bunch to whip the stud out and away from and then haze the bunch in with his own. That's usually quite an undertaking for a stud that already has a bunch, for the mares of the whipped ruler have their own ideas and might try to decide against the new one. They'd cause him a lot of trouble and would need a lot of hazing before they go his way and do as he wished. But there's nothing more ferocious in both looks and action than a hazing stallion. He won't stand for no argument and gets plenty rough, and sooner or later the mares do as he wishes whether they like it or him or not.

But the trouble is not all over even then, for after acquiring the new bunch there's the job of putting 'em in with the bunch he already has, and neither sides will agree to that, not for quite a spell and until the stallion does quite a bit more subduing and strong persuading. There's jealousy and fighting between the two bunches and the stallion has to set that to rights too. That takes quite a while, but after some hide is peeled off the orneriest one's rumps and a few swift kicks sets 'em to behaving and agreeing there's very little more trouble. The job is done. The harem is together, and now all there is to watch out for is that some other stallion doesn't come along and tries to spoil it all.

There's nothing more ferocious in both looks and action than a hazing stallion

It's a mystery as to how much power and endurance a wild stallion can have at them times. Such a big job may be no more than done when, if necessary, and another challenging stallion comes along, he's ready to dig right in and go it all over again, like never tiring.

Such an undertaking is just what the fiery young stud was going to try that day, to conquer and add on more mares to his harem. He was fresh and bold and mighty warrior-like as he left his small bunch to stand and came on the separating distance of about five hundred yards to challenge and meet the "good natured" old stud of the bunch Colonel, Charro and the two renegades was with.

The sleepy acting old stud watched the showy younger one come for a ways, then he sort of woke up, shook his heavy maned neck and trotted out to meet him. The colts and renegades tagged along, this time more like to watch the fun than to join in the battle. The mares stayed where they was and just watched.

It seems like there's no age limit as to a wild stallion's strength and fighting ability. The older they get the wickeder and more dangerous they are. Their hide and muscles seem to get tougher, and even tho sometimes, after losing their teeth, can easy enough whip young husky studs.

This good natured acting older stud showed the marks of many battles. He'd won more than he'd lost, and he'd learned that no matter how good he might be there was always some that could be still better. That was one thing the younger stallion hadn't as yet learned.

Leaving their bunches the way they did, to meet in the center, was something like two boxers leaving their corners for the center of the ring. The two stallions, one going easy but confident and the other bold and showy was like some boxers as they size up while coming for one another and then meet.

But there was no sparring as the two stallions met, they came on and clashed, and there was no clinching afterwards either. Like all fighters, wild stallions each

have their own style of fighting. The younger one came
on with knees up and forward, like a man might use his
elbows. That was to bump his opponent off balance so's
to get past his head and fasten his teeth along his neck
or throat. The older one came on, head up and as tho
to meet that, but he of a sudden wasn't there when the
young one rushed, so all bent to exterminate him right
quick. His knees couldn't find him, instead he found
himself sailing along the slope of his shoulder, lifted off
the ground, then a sharp pain of tearing hide along his
flank. That's where the older one's head had ducked to
and git for, to gut him. That was one of his styles of
fighting, and before the younger one had slid on past
him and got his balance that older one turned and fast-
ened his powerful jaws on the back of the younger one's
neck, paralyzing and dazing him.

The fight didn't last long after that. Quicker than the
the eye could see and while the younger one was still
dazed the older one switched holts, this time to the back
of his jaw and at his throat. It was a wonder he didn't
rip it wide open, and all that saved the younger stallion
there was that he'd been hit too hard, and he went down.

A horse doesn't hang on to his holt when the other is
up, and as the younger one went down, out of wind, the
older one let go, stomped him on the neck a couple of
times, dazing him some more.

He showed no more interest in him after that. He
raised his head high, let out a snorting nicker of victory,
and then his attention went to the younger stud's mares
that was still standing where they'd been left.

He shook his heavy maned neck and trotted towards

'em, and there wasn't even a soft howdedo nicker as he came near. He just proudly circled around 'em a couple of times, then he curved his neck down, held his head straight, level to within a few inches of the ground, and ears back, eyes full of fire, made a mighty wicked looking sight, the likes of which reminds mustang runners of a powerful snake ready to strike.

The mares knew that threatening sign. It was time for them to move, and that little bunch didn't want to argue with that wicked one, for they'd seen him in action.

The mares was hazed past their fallen ruler and on to join the victor's bunch. That was the result of the battle, the younger cocksure warrior losing all instead of acquiring more, besides being badly chewed and gashed up.

But he'd got off lucky even at that, he was still alive, the gashes would heal and he'd soon enough come back to fighting mood again, try to whip some other stud out of his bunch and now all the wiser as to how to go about it. He wouldn't leave himself wide open again when he'd rush, and depend altogether on his strength and weight as he had.

The older stud didn't try to move his now good sized bunch on after he'd hazed in the new appropriated mares. He just stayed out to one side of 'em and lapped crusted snow while keeping an eye on his opponent which now had raised his head and would soon be up. For he might want to go on with the battle, as some do, and try to get his harem back, and the older stud was prepared in case he did.

But there was no such intentions in the younger one's

mind right then as he struggled up to his feet, and as he got a glimpse of the older one starting after him again, there was no more show of warrior about him. He done his best to get away as fast as he could, and his legs, even tho shaky, was still good. The old stud hazed him out on his way, just to make sure, and then returned to his bunch. The sleepy looking, good natured old stud had more than surprised the two wise renegades and gave Colonel and Charro something to watch out for when it come to fighting. In that battle he'd of a sudden won their admiration and respect, they wasn't to be fooled by his sleepy look and easy going ways no more.

But, as it goes, that no matter how good one may be there's always another just as good or still better, that went on to be proved some time later.

Before then there come a few skirmishes with mustang runners, and there was where the two wise renegades came in and done more than their share to help lead the bunch from hard runs, traps and to clean getaways. For a spell, and figuring the wild ones to be weak from the first warm days of the coming spring, mustangers got to pop up here and there pretty often, but there was too many wise heads steady a watching in the old stud's bunch for it to be rode up onto unawares, and that bunch having been on good range all winter was far from being weak. At the first sight of a mustanger or of some other running bunch showing there was one near, the renegades would lead on for the roughest of country, a country they'd know well and where they would soon vanish from sight.

When that spell of mustangers' skirmishes was over for the time and the bunch got to grazing more at ease again only a few of the mares was missing, some that was too heavy with foal to go on, and others, young rattle-brained fillies of the age when they think they're too smart to follow the lead of the wise ones.

But even with that loss there was still a fair sized bunch kept together when spring really did come, melting snows leaving puddles and pools of water in many places, and with bunch grass greening up on the rough hillsides and hollows.

It was while enjoying this peace and plenty of spring-time one day that a tornado, in the shape of a regular devil horse hit the bunch, with no warning, and scattered it from there to yonder. The old stud had been the first one hit and bowled over, the two renegades lost some hide in getting away, and by that time Colonel and Charro had been wise enough to skeedaddle away from there quick.

Right smack on top of that and going right on, the mares was slam-banged into a quick run, hazed over a ridge and out of sight, while the scattered remaining ones could only look on, trying to get their wits to-gether. It all happened so sudden that none realized at the time what was really happening, and when they finally come to, looking at one another like to take count on how many of 'em was left and if all in one piece, they still felt sort of confused, for that devil horse must of been part thunderbolt as well as tornado the way he was everywhere at once and done his work so quick and smooth.

The old stud had been the first one hit and bowled over

The two renegades had seen many battles and much scattering of bunches but never like this one, and, looking at the old stud down below 'em, standing and just looking around some, he was also like wondering what had happened, but seemed none the worse for what did happen. It had been too sudden.

And now, counting noses, there was only five of 'em left, kind of scattered as yet, but they got together again and begin drifting some, for none felt like grazing for a spell, and Colonel, having never witnessed anything like that before, was spooky and still wide eyed at the suddenness and of what all it had been about.

As the small bunch drifted old stud lagged on behind, like wondering which way to go. For he wasn't satisfied to be with only the geldings and the colts, he'd rather be alone for a spell. But he did drift along with 'em for a ways and grazed with 'em for a spell, until the dark of that night come, then, after a short rest, he started out, alone.

He'd ramble on and take it easy for some days, maybe weeks. By that time he'd be on his summer range, where few mustangers ever bothered him, and there he'd in time find a likely bunch with a stud he could whip out and then all would be at peace again, excepting for as usual watching out for other studs and other things a wild stallion has to steady keep watch for.

CHAPTER THIRTEEN

SHE WAS THE CAUSE OF IT ALL

WITH the coming of that spring, Colonel was now a three year old, round and fat as a butter ball, and restless as an aspen leaf. He'd hardly put his head down for a tuft of bunch grass when it'd be up again and looking all around while he chewed on it. He'd walk on a ways for no seeming reason and back again, but a fair reason then. For Colonel had taken on responsibility, responsibility in the trim shape of a two year old filly.

He didn't have to fight no stud to get her and he didn't steal her out of no bunch. She'd just come along, like lost, alone, and he'd just appropriated her. There'd been no fuss about it and she'd right away went to grazing and running close by his side and plum contented.

As luck would have it, he'd been grazing well away from Charro and the other two when he first spotted the filly, and out of curiosity more than anything else he'd trotted out to meet her. It had been love at first sight, and now for fear of losing her and thru pure jealousy he didn't go back to his running pardners with her but kept her away from them as much as he could.

But them wise ones soon enough spotted him in the .distance, and noticing there was a stranger with him they all three trotted up to investigate. There was no use trying to get away, and when the three surrounded the filly, in also wanting to make an acquaintance with her,

Colonel had taken on responsibility, responsibility in the trim shape of a two year old filly

was the first time that Colonel ever set his ears back at them or showed any sign that they wasn't welcome to be near.

He tried to stand between her and them but they didn't pay no attention to him, and when he nipped Charro on the neck for getting too close he was as surprised at the act as Charro was. Then he nipped one of the renegades, that surprised that wise one too, and like to make fun of the colt, that he shouldn't be silly, he just landed a light kick on his ribs and let it go at that.

But at last and when their curiosity was satisfied and the acquaintance of the filly was made they left him be, with his first love, and went on to grazing, cocking their ears at him and blowing their noses like as much as to say, "Gee, aint love grand."

Whether it was love and it was grand, Colonel sure acted strange since the filly came along. He was like in a trance and had eyes only for her. He'd of course once in a while glance towards his pardners and follow along wherever they went, for he didn't want to lose track of them either. But, while in the open, him and his lady love would keep a mile or so away from them, seldom getting closer than half a mile, even in the rough country.

It was sort of queer the way Colonel had got so taken up with the filly. He'd run with bunches where there was many of 'em and he'd paid no attention to 'em, no more than just another horse. But this slim sorrel filly wasn't like any of them. She'd sort of stirred something in him, like from away in the past, when a young colt in the blue grass country, a faint feeling that she was like the ones he used to play with them, not like these mustang ones he'd been running with. Maybe she had the same feeling towards him, that she understood his kind and not the wild ones.

How she came to be in that country alone was a mystery that didn't at all worry Colonel in trying to figure out. All he felt was that she was more like him than any horse he'd ever been with since leaving his mother's side, maybe of the same breed, the kind he'd been taken away from, and now that was what might of drawed him to her. One thing sure, she could run, the only one he'd seen that could near keep up with him. But there was another thing he also noticed, she wasn't wise to the wild horse country, and now he took it onto himself to teach and watch over her as Charro had over him. That is, as much as he could like Charro had.

But as the two would wander away so far from the three wise ones they would of been very easy pickings for a mustanger. Here was a chance that Blackie would sure liked to 've had. But as good luck would have it there was few mustangers out at the time, especially in that part of the country. So they grazed and roamed along in bliss, still keeping track of the three wise ones, and also their distance.

Then one day, after a couple of weeks of such bliss, there come a rider, a rider who with only his head showing above the top of a high ridge first spotted three horses a mile or so below him, them three was Charro and the two renegades, and then, about the same distance from them, was two more horses. The rider leveled his field glasses on them, and then a long pleased grin spread over his face. Then a puzzled expression come, for he couldn't figure out that sorrel with the brown, and leveling his glasses on the three horses, he couldn't figure out the grulla not being with them. That brown being apart from the grulla and with the sorrel instead was what puzzled him.

He pondered on that for quite a spell, and then the grin of a sudden came back, now even more pleased than before. It had all come to him as plain as day, and he couldn't of wished for anything to be more in his favor than they was right then.

Knowing horses as he did, especially the brown and the grulla, he knew what had happened about as well as if he'd been right on the spot, that the two colts had separated and the reason why, also that the brown still didn't want to be separated too far from the grulla. That's what he'd work on, and he'd have to work it just right or this good chance would be spoiled.

The brown was the one the rider wanted, and knowing that it'd be about impossible to get him if he was to get in with the grulla and the other two again. He seen where it'd be best to spook them three out of that country first, and without the brown noticing, if possible, for if he did he'd be very apt to want to join them, and with that speed of his there'd be no stopping nor turning him from doing that.

Of course there was still the sorrel to consider. That one might be pretty hard to handle too, but the rider would figure on some chance with that one where he wouldn't if the brown got in with the grulla.

Sizing up the country below, the rider seen where luck was with him some more, for in the mile space between the two bunches was a couple of strings of long ridges high enough to well block the view from one to the other.

Now was to keep out of sight of the brown and the sorrel while getting to the other three. So, picking his way around, he got off his horse until he got over the tall ridge he was on, then struck down a deep gully, which would of been better going for mountain goats than man and horse, but he was out of sight of the horses there and seen where it led on down in between the long ridges below, where he'd be out of sight of both bunches.

The distance to the horses was covered mighty careful and quiet, and when the rider figured he was even between the two bunches he rode to the side of one of the benches so he could only look over it, not showing himself. He spotted the three he wanted to spook away and then getting to within as short distance as he could he then spurted up to their full sight sudden, like him and his horse had just shot up from the earth, and rode full speed towards 'em.

The so sudden appearance of the rider more than done the trick and the three didn't hesitate as to where they should go, they just up and went, like the devil was on their tail, and straight away from the other two, for rough foothills and rougher country above.

There was no use chasing them on, for after the scare they had they'd keep on running until they was well out of the country. The rider watched 'em go for quite a while, and when they was only small dots bobbing over distant ridges now and again and finally entirely disappeared he rode the opposite direction and where the other two had been. Now would be the real ticklish work, depended a whole lot on the sorrel. He knew the brown would make a dash for where he figured Charro and the other two to be, and finding them gone he'd be pretty well confused and lost as to where to go. Then would be the time to get 'em going towards some of the blind traps which the country was full of in some parts. He could tell better which way to try to head 'em after he seen how the sorrel acted, that one might spoil everything and be as hard to turn or as wise as the grulla and the other two.

The only thing to do was to ride towards 'em slow and not spook 'em any more than was possible. Let 'em take their own course for a spell, then he'd know better as to how to proceed to run 'em.

The rider had figured right. As he slowly rode up on the two and stopped his horse they raised their heads, stood like petrified for a second, then the brown started into a lead the sorrel only following. That lead hadn't been of the spooky jump and tight run of the wild horse but just in a long easy lope, like mighty confident they could outrun the rider if need be.

But that rider didn't make no effort to run or try to turn 'em any direction. He'd just poked along and watched 'em while the brown led in a circle to get to the bunch of three he'd been keeping track of and running with before he'd took up with the filly.

The rider had expected that and knew there'd been no use trying to stop him from making that run in look-ing for his ex-pardners. Trying to do that would only made him worse.

An now when the brown come to where he'd last seen his pardners and there was no sign of 'em nowheres he

liked to went wild, nickering, running in big circles from
knoll to knoll and ridge to ridge looking for 'em, but
only in that neighboring part. But them three was
many miles away from there by then, where he'd never
be apt to find 'em again if he looked for 'em for a
month. The rider had seen to that.

Now, with the many long circling runs of looking for
them the brown was mighty confused, and another thing,
the filly had quit following him, just sort of stood in one
place watching him making his long searching circles,
appearing here and disappearing there, only to appear
again and come back to her.

The rider had got off his horse on a high knoll during
the proceedings, and from there, watching all from a
good distance he seen that again luck was sure with him,
for that sorrel filly was not a wild one but as as gentle
breeding as the brown originally was. What was more he
seen from her actions that she hadn't been amongst the
wild ones for very long, that the brown wouldn't leave
her, and that way the two could now be driven right on
wherever wished the same as any gentle bred horses they
really was. The filly wouldn't run from a rider, and soon
as the brown had his good run and cooled down some
they'd be no trouble.

And there was no trouble, only some mighty ticklish
work in getting the brown to quieting down and not go to
out running the rider as he had before, just for the fun
of it and show he could do it. But the filly had most all
to do in quieting him down, for when he'd start on one
of his spurts she'd just trot a ways and soon enough he'd

come back. The rider stayed well behind and sort of out of sight at such times, for he knew better than try to run him.

It went on being ticklish for the rider that way until well out of the wild horse country and around the point of the last badland ridge, and such an experienced rider as that one was all that'd made that feat possible.

There was four days of steady riding for that rider since he'd started the two and only two nights' stops, that was when the edge of the big valley was reached and the brown got to behaving so him and the filly could be corralled, and then on the fourth day come sight of the Hip-O ranch when now the brown, Colonel, perked his ears and again stretched out on his lead, this time only to a good steady walk towards it.

There would be a couple of weeks before Brad would be hitting out with the rodeo stock. There was still plenty of riding to be done near and away from the ranch in the meantime, and one day, while riding near the ranch, Virginia rode up alongside of him. She was riding Colonel.

Colonel's long spell of freedom amongst wild ones hadn't made any changes in his actions, only physical, which was considerable improved and developed. But the day Brad had run him into the corral after getting him from the wild horse country he'd walked up to him and only acted pleased to see him close again, the same as the year before he got away and as tho that time of wild freedom had been only for a space of fun. Now that that was over, there was no trace of wildness about him, and when the happy Virginia walked into the corral a little later he nickered and came to meet her the same as before and as he always had while at the ranch.

He well showed his long line of gentle breeding that way, but another year or so of the wild freedom as he'd had and it might of been different. He might of been still gentle if caught but there'd been a considerable loss of interest for the human, that interest would of been more for freedom and, as some do, get plenty mean.

Colonel didn't get to that stage. He was still the kind, gentle and willing colt when Brad brought him in the second time as he'd ever been, when once in the corral, and when Virginia again slipped her saddle on and rode him only a few days afterwards he acted as tho it had been just the day before since she'd done so.

As for the sorrel filly, which was really Colonel's "downfall," or the cause of his being caught, there wasn't so much thought spent on her. She looked like a very well bred filly and, as Virginia laughed, good company for Colonel and not at all the kind that would lead him out to some wild bunch as Charro had. Little Charro wasn't missed much on that account. Besides, all knew he'd sure take care of himself well.

Virginia again took Colonel to hand and went to ride him oftener and harder than before. It wasn't that she wanted to punish him for his second running away but just that he now could stand much more riding, and she figured him to be at a good age, when a horse learns best, if not rode too hard. Virginia wasn't one to ride any horse too hard, and now she wanted to teach him what she'd started out to the year before. That was pay attention to cattle, outdodge 'em instead of wanting to run straight on and pass everything, to watch a rope and prepare for a jerk, to stop and hold the rope tight when a critter is down, and all that goes on with cow work.

She told Brad about that one day, of her troubles in teaching him any such, and remarking that her dad only laughed at her for trying, she asked him if he would try the colt out on just a good yearling to see if he'd ever get next to pay attention to the rope and the yearling at the other end instead of just running on like he was in a race track. There was other things along other lines with range work she wanted to have Brad try him on, and see if there was any hopes for him to ever be a good cowhorse, or maybe a good rope horse to use in arenas during rodeos.

At all of that, Brad had to laugh too. But one time, and to please her he did get on Colonel and tried him. He tried him well, amongst a good bunch of cattle, at roping and at what most everything a cowhorse should do, and the only result was Brad's shaking of his head as he rode him out of the herd. Virginia had of course witnessed it all and had to agree with him.

What Brad had always kept to himself was the fine breeding of Colonel and for what purpose. He'd seen and broke well bred horses that turned out to be fine cowhorses, but even tho he'd said so he'd never had no intentions of making any such out of Colonel. For that pony was from too long and good a strain of track horses to expect him to ever be anything else but that. He had

Virginia again took Colonel to hand

no especial reason to buy him as a colt excepting he just wanted him, maybe Virginia would like him too. But back of it all was a hunch and Brad went strong on hunches— Then, after the deal was clinched there come sight of the colt's pedigree, and at that he felt his hunch had sure started right.

As Brad and Virginia rode back to the ranch, Brad says to her. "You've rode this colt quite a while. That is, enough so's to know if he has the natural knack it takes to make a cowhorse. You could tell that after a few rides of your own horses when you broke them, and with all the rides you've given Colonel do you think he has the makings to ever match any in your string?"

Virginia had to laugh a little. "Why no." she says "He goes by a cow so fast he never sees her, and if one would ever happen to be in his way I'm sure he'd run right over her. No, as a cowhorse he'll never do, but as for speed he would make a jack rabbit ashamed of itself."

Brad now had to laugh at her good describing of Colonel's failings and qualities. Finally he said.

"The first rodeo I have on hand is only a couple of hundred miles away. Why not let's take Colonel and try him in a race there?"

"It would be all right, I guess." says Virginia, wondering "But who's going to ride him?"

Brad smiled at her again and said, "You are——"

CHAPTER FOURTEEN

WHITEWASHED

THIS race was to be a fair sized one. Horses much above the average was entered from all parts of the state, and some still better from other states. There was good stakes and high betting. Not much betting on Colonel, for nobody knew him.

Virginia had of course never rode in a race before and neither had Colonel been in such. The girl was a little nervous as to that but Brad eased her some, got her a box stall to one quiet end of the stable, fitted her up with good jockey garb and a young colored groom to fix up Colonel, and sort of coached her some.

With all of that she got to feeling pretty confident. She rode Colonel around the track a couple of times, not at his full speed but just to make him acquainted with it, and let him know what was wanted of him. Besides she herself wanted to get acquainted with that postage stamp-size piece of pigskin which was called a saddle and she was supposed to ride on, also the stirrups so short that her knees near touched her chin.

There was three races at that rodeo, going on between the events of bronc-riding, steer riding, bull-dogging, etc. Virginia and Colonel was up for the third race, and when that time come, Brad was the one who led Colonel on the track and put him in his starting place. That eased Virginia a considerable, and even tho Colonel was cool acting, all excepting for his first sight of so many people he behaved like the sensible horse he was.

One of the main things with him, Brad knew, would be the start—to start along with them crazy acting, experienced race horses around him.

But that was partly taken care of, for as Brad watched the race starter and in time gave the sign, Brad like a flash slapped Colonel along the flank and on the rump, and with the other horses starting so quick on both sides of him Colonel was only his own half a length behind when the race began.

Then the fun begin, fun for Colonel mostly, for he was running with other horses that really could run, with riders on 'em, and to him he got the same pleasure as he had in outdistancing and playing with the riders while on the wild horse range.

He kept abreast of some of the few leaders for a spell, like as if to find out if they could run with him. And then when two riders sort of shouldered against his neck and tried to pinch him out is when, with the coaching of Virginia, the race really did begin. Colonel no more than got pinched back, and got in the clear on the outside of 'em when he left the riders like they was riding hobbled horses. Favorites and well known horses was passed on the same way (it was a mile race). Colonel was now playing with and getting away from them riders the same as he had played and got away from the mustangers, and when he crossed the line, head up like a wild horse instead of a race horse, there was so many horse lengths behind him that if they'd been flesh there'd been enough to call it a herd.

Old Cal had been on the job to see that rodeo and race and his old racing spirit more than revived as he watched Colonel come to the line like he did. He was hard to hold down for a spell, and when Brad got to tell him there was another rodeo a few weeks off and not so far away from this one, Old Cal bounced up and says.

"Me and Virginia'll sure be there. We'll drive this time and I'll bring that good horse trailer to put Colonel in so he won't be jammed around in them stock cars amongst other horses."

"Don't you worry about Colonel. He gets less jamming around in the box cars I put him in than he would in a trailer. I got a partition for him the same as I had when I first brought him to the ranch, when he was a little feller, and no jars nor other horse can bother him."

About the same horses, jockeys, race horse fans and betters was there at that second rodeo (Rodeos includes horse races but it's called Rodeo) There'd been heavy losses with playing the favorites when this unknown dark horse, Colonel, coming in so far aheard and so easy, and now, with this second rodeo race he was of a sudden twenty to one the favorite.

At seeing Colonel again up for the race the owners of race horses got together and made a beller to the judges against letting him run as he was a thoroughbred.* Cal happened along about then.

*(There wasn't supposed to be over three-quarter bloods in such races).

Colonel was now playing with and getting away from them riders the same
as he had played and got away from the mustangers

"Thoroughbred me eye" he chips in why that horse's been with wild horses for two years anyway, and we been trying to cach him all that time. Figure that out."

The judges grinned and looked at the squawkers. Then one of 'em says. "Supposing he is a thoroughbred. I happen to know that three of you sneaked in registered horses yourselves, so better keep quiet."

Then there was talk of handicapping Colonel. Old Cal doubled up in a laughing fit at that. "Why you could put an extra hundred pounds on him, put him on a muddy track alongside of yours on a dry one and he'll still fan his tail in your ponies' faces."

Brad was over at the Rodeo grounds, by the chutes, while all this was going on, and after laughing at what Cal told him of it, he got to thinking. That horse is too much for the smaller races. First thing he knew they wouldn't let him enter him. It never even entered his mind to have the horse "pulled" (held back). That would spoil a horse with such a heart as Colonel's. The only thing he got to decide on would be to take to bigger races. But that would have to be apart from his rodeo work.

Then he finally got to figuring. Being he had contracts far and wide for rodeos he'd use Colonel in such ones where that horse wasn't known. It wouldn't take long of course when he would be well known, but Brad thought that by being careful he could get by that summer until fall, and the races Colonel would be having would be great training to him in preparing for the bigger races.

At this second rodeo, Colonel outdistanced the other horses even more than before, for then he'd already learned to be ready and going from the start, not like the first when Brad had to slap him to going.

There was no more pleased nor tickled girl than Virginia after so easy winning the second race, but near as sad a girl when that rodeo was over and Cal said it was time to pack up the car and hit back home for the ranch. The next rodeo Brad had to go on was some five hundred miles away, and he would take Colonel with him.

In his tall figuring, Brad had forgot that Colonel was Virginia's horse. He'd have to talk his plans over with her and of course ask her permission to take him.

The three walked to the hotel. Cal had his say as to how pleased he was about the second race. Then seeing how Brad and Virginia begin talking of the future plans for Colonel, the dividing of the winnings and such, and Cal not wanting to get mixed up with that, stopped packing his bag, throwed up his hands and hit downstairs for the hotel bar to talk with other horsemen about the race and what a horse his daughter had. That Colonel horse.

"These rodeos I've got on hand from now on, Brad went on to say to Virginia after Cal left "are quite some distance away and far apart. You and your dad couldn't very well follow them, and, Virginia, I would sure like to take Colonel alone. You can bet your boots he'll get the best of care and the best of riders. You've seen how the track is in his blood, also found out he'd never be a cow-horse, he's not bred for that.

"With his speed there'd be some great winnings made at every rodeo, also outside races, and to make it fair and interesting I'll do the handling of him and split the winnings with you."

With her hands between her knees, Virginia only stared at the floor as he spoke, Brad watching her every expression. He knew she didn't want to part with Colonel, even if only for the summer months. He also knew she didn't give a whoop for any share or all the winnings. There was something else in her expression which was away beyond him to understand. It was no thoughts of the horse and sure no thoughts of the winnings, he knew. It was more as a yearning for something that for the lack of understanding there was very little hope of getting.—If she would only speak.

To get to the bottom of that last, Brad again brought up the subject which he figured she sort of resented but might bring her to talk on what he couldn't understand. It was about the winnings.

"If you don't feel right about only half the winnings for your share," he begins, as a stir up "I'll give you all and keep only the entrance fees, expenses for the groom and my general superiv——."

At that point she turned her face at him, and a glance of her large expressive moist eyes did not surprise him. They told what he already knew, but what did surprise him was that they told she knew how he himself cared but didn't speak.

It was sometime afterwards when the door flew open and Old Cal, feeling pretty good, caught the two sitting side by side close, one arm around each other, both free hands clasped and heads together.

Cal stared in surprise for a few seconds then a long pleased grin spread over his face.

"I knew it," he says, "I knew it would happen soon as my back was turned, and I turned it apurpose." Then to Brad "you sure know how to pick winners. Virginia ain't so bad at that either. Now I see you had to get her in order to get Colonel. But she'll most likely take care of the winnings—But here, children." He took the hand of each and layed 'em one on top of the other, and holding 'em that way, he went on. "It ain't for an old sinner like me to say such things but God bless you both, and I wish you all the happiness you two sure enough deserve."

With the goings on of every Rodeo, Colonel was put thru the paces with the races that went along with 'em, Virginia, now Mrs. Braddock, as his jockey, who, with every race got very wise to the tricks of the game, such as being crowded to the rail, held back by horses ahead, being pinched in and so on. With such a horse as Colonel she didn't try to at first hit for the inside and crowd the rail. Instead she kept clear of all other riders from the start, took the outside, and it wasn't long when she'd be well in the lead and have the track and rail by herself the rest of the stretch to the line.

Her and Brad would grin at one another sort of sheepish after each race, for it seemed a shame to take the money. The consolation they'd get would be the surprise and cheer of the crowds.

The name, Colonel, got so spread and looked for on

the programs that for fear the horse would be barred from the race on account of his super speed Brad went to changing the horse's name at every race he was entered in. But many race fans had got to know that horse and that made it even better for them to lay heavy bets on him, for the names would of course be unknown. To them who knew him by sight he got to be called the "Dark Horse."

But regardless of the name changing, Brad had a hard time entering Colonel by the time fall come and the rodeo season was over.

Brad and Virginia honeymooned at the ranch that winter, in an ell of the big ranch house. Red had to remark about that, that he'd have to mend his ways too, save his money and find the girl. That was quite some program for Red, but the big stump would be to find the place.

Jim was satisfied to stay being the lone wolf. But he would sure like to get enough money together so he could buy a silver-mounted, diamond-studded bridle bit he'd seen. The price was a thousand dollars.

Brad didn't get to cross the mountains and go to contesting along the coast on south that winter. Virginia wouldn't let him for one thing, and another, he didn't want to. He hadn't been allowed to contest no more since the knot was tied. His job from then was to keep charge of the bucking stock, arena directing, keep an eye on Colonel and, all his time outside of that, on Virignia. But she'd sometimes take pity on him and let him get in on roping contests.

While riding together that winter, breaking trail for snowbound cattle, bringing in the weaker stock to the feed grounds, there was of course many things talked about, about the future. Brad was for starting a ranch of his own, with good cattle and horses and quit following the rodeos entirely, remarking it was no life he wanted her to follow, that he'd had enough of it himself and so on.

But there was no quitting just like that, and so, when spring and summer came on again, Brad, Red and Jim went on with the stock as usual, and to fill the contracts that'd been made for the different Rodeos. Virginia was of course right alongside of Brad and caring for Colonel.

Many a track fan who knew the "Dark Horse" by sight kept looking for him at the rodeo races that summer, for, to them, no matter what his name might be changed to he was like a gold mine, for it was easy to get a twenty to one bet on him from others who didn't know him, being the name would most always be a strange one at each Rodeo.

But to the disappointment of them many there came no sight of that wonder, the "Dark Horse." There was one horse tho that fooled as many as the "Dark Horse" had. This one was built the same as him and had the same way of hitting the line from five to ten lengths ahead of the other horses in every race, and "you'd of swore he was the 'Dark Horse,'" only this one had big white spots on shoulder and thigh and a full blazed face. He could near be classed as a pinto.

Then again, there was another horse of near the same color, size, and action as the "Dark Horse" that fooled many who played him as being that "Dark Horse."

"You'd of swore he was the 'Dark Horse,'" only this one had big white spots on shoulder and thigh and a full blazed face

Heavy bets was layed on him but he'd usually come in along between fourth and last.

The Pinto, or Paint, as the fast one got to be called soon made a reputation that spread, and no matter if his name was changed them spots was what the betters bet on.

But them spots wasn't like the leopard's, for they could be changed, washed off, and under them was the dark brown hide of the Dark Horse, Colonel.

Virginia had nothing to do in this "dark" conspiracy,

in fact she didn't like the idea of what she felt was cheating in changing Colonel's name, much less to turning him into a pinto. Brad and Red was the guilty parties there, and after Brad explained to her why he changed the horse in both names and color, that it was so he could enter him in the races, with no idea of cheating any one, she then didn't object no more. If anything she was willing to help, for, like Brad, she felt that Colonel was too good a horse to be left idle, just on account of his goodness.

In realizing and wanting to help that way she would change from one outfit to another. When she rode Colonel as the "Dark Horse" she rode as a jockey of course but with her hair a flying as a girl, and when she rode him as the Pinto she darkened her fair hair and complexion, shoved her tresses under her cap and, at a distance, looked all for the world like a sunburnt jockey. The costumes was changed too, and being the races was days and sometimes weeks apart that was more pleasure for her than effort.

As for Brad and Red putting the spots on Colonel or taking 'em off, that was no hard work either, all they had to do was mix a little thin whitewash and with a fine spray of that plant the spots where they wanted 'em. If they wanted Colonel as he naturally was afterwards a little water and a sponge would easy take them spots off.

So easy that sometimes, while Virginia would be riding him in such disguise she'd be mighty worried of threatening showers and a muddy track—There was one time when a good shower did come during a race while Colonel was spotted up and she was darkened up, and before the line was reached the dark of her face was running down her shirt and the white spots on Colonel washed off into the mud. She didn't waste no time by the judges or welcoming crowd that day.

Along with the rodeos that play went on for that year. There was a couple of times when Colonel wasn't allowed to be entered, and a few times when he was recognized, spots or no spots, and he was allowed to come in, but only for the reason that the officials knew there'd be a safe bet on that horse and a good chance for them to make a stake——

Red would always put all he had on him, take all bets he could get and he figured that if this kept up he'd soon be able to buy a good already running outfit, if he hung on to that money, and then get the girl.

Brad "invested" that way too, careful not to let Virginia know, and he'd made many times over the four hundred dollars he'd paid for Colonel when he'd bought him as a colt. Jim also throwed in his chips and got that silver-mounted, diamond-incrusted bridle bit he wanted.

All in all everything went well, quite a few track slickers was turned into whitewashed suckers, and as Colonel, along with the bucking stock was shipped back to the ranch that fall, he was in fine condition, had good track experience, and was rearing to go on some more.

CHAPTER FIFTEEN

THE BREED OF 'EM

WITH the rush of the late fall works, along with the beef round-up and shipping the boys had no more than got to the ranch with the rodeo stock when they had to jump right in and go to work on the range. Cal had already started the works with the boys that had been kept steady on the outfit, and he'd hired two more to take the place of Brad, for, as there'd need to be a rider at the ranch to ride from there he'd decided, now that Brad was a married man, to let him have that job. Him and Virginia could handle things.

So, as Cal and his riders went to rounding up on the range, Brad and Virginia went to scouring the hills close to the ranch. Virginia went back to her regular range clothes, which felt mighty good, and her stock saddle again, and her string of ponies which had got mighty fat and rollicky.

With all the range work to be done, Colonel wasn't neglected. It was too late in the year for pasturing but he had the freedom of the big corral, shed and box stall of nights. Virginia rode him now and again, just to sort of keep his spirits in good shape, but there never come no more thoughts to her mind of trying to make a cow-horse out of him. She didn't put him to no range work,

just a good run and a rub down, and she didn't care no
more now if he did pass a cow without seeing 'er while
going thru his paces.

As good a care as that horse'd had while at the ranch
since he was a colt it was near impossible that he could
be getting more, but he was, and kept in as fine a trim
and shape as any horse could be kept. He could of been
jumped out of the stable any time and been ready for
any race.

With all of that, care and all, adding on his long
spells of wild freedom which developed his body, stamina,
heart and courage, the sure handling of his long legs
and all which he couldn't of got in any training stables,
and with his breeding to go with that it was no wonder
he was a super horse, and now that he'd had a couple
of summers on the track for the finishing touches,
well——

It was along about middle winter when Cal, who'd
been receiving race track news which was kept being
sent to him, telling of the outcome of the latest races
and the announcing of them that was to come, perked
up his ears at one such news report. It was of a big race
that was to be pulled off acrost the mountains to the
coast. The stake was for fifty thousand dollars. But
what made Cal perk his ears was that amongst them who
entered some horses was a Morgan Mansfield.

Cal led out a warwhoop, hunted up Brad and pointing a finger at the name he could hardly speak for excitement.

"There's an old enemy of mine," he says. "He crooked me out of two races. Of course I don't hold that against him because there's no holds barred in races, like with love or war. But we're going to take in that race, and with Colonel we'll skin him out of his pants."

It was hard for Brad to keep a straight face and his mouth shut at surprise of the sight of Mansfield's name and then at what Cal was aiming to do to him. The race would be for four year olds. Mansfield had entered two of 'em, and it came to Brad that they would be Colonel's half-brothers.

Cal was happy as a kid with stick candy at the prospect of getting back at Mansfield after so many years. While with Brad, he was a little dubious.

It was the next day when Brad came to Cal and asked. "What are you going to do for a jockey? You know without me telling you that there's no lady jockeys in such races. Besides, she couldn't go." He talked low into Cal's ear, and at that Cal's eyes near popped out with surprise, then a long pleased grin spread over his face as he gripped Brad's hand and says: "Congratulations, my boy, congratulations. God bless your hide."

But the jockey matter was a serious one, and Cal paced the floor some that evening and wrinkled his brows on the subject. Then, like the sun breaking thru the clouds, it came to him.

The roads was hardly fit for automobiles on account of deep snow drifts, but Cal put on his heavy skid chains and hit out as tho he was skimming along on a boulevard. When he seen a bad drift ahead he put the spurs to the powerful motor, and the way he drove it would of took an ice berg to 've stopped him.

He made it into town and in front of the telephone office in good skidding shape. There he called for long distance, to the warden of the State Prison. There was a long confab between him and that warden, and when he walked out of that office there was a very satisfied look on his face.

It would be about three months before the big race would take place. A jockey should get acquainted with the horse he's to ride and the horse acquainted with him, and the training. Then there was the transportation to be considered. So, a month before the time for the race, Cal drove some hundred miles to the State Prison to see the warden there. There was another confab and after a spell a grinning little feller bearing a number was shaking hands with Cal. It was Blackie.

The warden spoke. "Well, Blackie," he says. "I'm going to let you go on your honor and in charge of our friend Cal Goodwin here. I know you won't break that trust." The warden leaned back on his chair and smiled at him. "I'm betting on you," he went on, "and not only you but on a good horse, to win. If you do win, or even if you dont but try, I'll see what I can do for you for a parole when you get back." He stood up, reached over the desk and shook hands with him. "I have faith in you, and good luck."

Then he looked at Cal with a half grin and a squint and says, "As for you, dont you ever come back to this state without him, and the winnings."

There was no happier or grateful a half-pint-size cowboy than Blackie as Cal drove him out to the ranch and turned Colonel over to him. That horse had led him on many a chase while on the wild horse range, sort of played with him and then run on, leaving him behind as tho he was tied. He'd cussed his hide many a time for that, all the while admiring him. And now, feeling and knowing the smooth power of him, he looked up at that horse, not only as a cause of relief from the iron bars but as one that'd lead others on a merry chase. Blackie would see to that.

Virginia didn't at all mind turning Colonel over to Blackie, for she felt and seen that with his care and handling the horse would do wonders, more than she'd ever done or could ever do herself, and that was going some.

There was a week or so of light training at the ranch, then Colonel was loaded into Cal's best horse trailer. Cal took the wheel at the car, and with Blackie beside him, the three hit for the now open mountain passes and for the track many hundred miles away, where the race was to be held. But not before Brad, Red, Jim, and some of the other boys dug up all they could for Cal to place on Colonel for them.

"You see, Blackie," says Cal as they started out, "we sure have got to win."

"Yes," says Blackie, "and I only wish I had something to chip in, too."

Cal grinned. "I'll stake you," he says.

After three days of driving, the track was finally

reached, a good big stall located and there Blackie made camp, right beside Colonel. He didn't want to go to no hotel and wouldn't trust no groom. Cal brought him his meals, and with his 45 six-shooter which he'd dug out of his war bag before leaving the ranch always kept right handy he et and slept right by Colonel.

The two weeks or so before the race was more than enjoyed by both man and horse. Blackie, very much used to night riding and in mighty rough countries wouldn't put Colonel to his good speed on the smooth track only at that time, when everybody was asleep. This was a sure enough "dark horse" and he didn't want no one to see him stretch on a run. In daytime he'd only lope him out a bit and then rub him down. Nobody paid much attention to either him or the horse, they was only a little curious, curious at a branded horse running in such a race and a cowboy looking feller as a jockey and who wouldn't mix with anybody.

During that time Cal had run Mansfield down. He was the boy he was after, and Mansfield remarking how Cal was sure a glutton for punishment covered all he wanted to bet. It was aplenty, and paying five to one to Cal's favor if he won.

The day of the race finally come, and Cal was on the job early that day to see that all was well with Blackie and Colonel, also to size the other horses again, especially Mansfield's. The spirit of the old racing days more than came back to him and he felt a mighty tense but pleased feeling as he'd return to take another look at Colonel. He felt it in his bones that he'd win.

seconds, like the quiet before the storm, the ponies was all in good line, and out went the starting flag, which acted as if a bombshell exploded behind each horse.

Colonel, being quiet, was a slow starter, but this time he started fairly good, only half a length behind the two crazy ones that had been on each side of him. Them two started out so fast they thought they had wings and forgot to use their legs, and about five lengths from the starting line rammed against one another and piled up, piled up right in front of Colonel.

Cool headed Colonel tried to jump the mix up but he was too close when it happened and he piled up, upended right on top of 'em.

A cloud of dust was stirred by the scrambling hoofs, but Cal could see the Mansfield ponies in the clear and hitting out. At that same time there come a heavy slap on his back and a roaring, laughing voice saying, "There goes your money, Cal old boy."

At the slap, and being tense, Cal bit his cigar in two, swallowing the part he had in his mouth. He couldn't and didn't want to speak for a spell, for even tho near choking his eyes was at the instant on Colonel which had fell in the heap a running, turned over and got up a running, with Blackie out of the saddle but right into it again (a feat that had never been witnessed before), and on with the race horse and rider went, leaving the other two riderless horses still scrambling to their feet.

Not many paid much attention to this unknown horse nor the other two—the Mansfield horses was well in the lead.

But the race was still young. Blackie stuck his nose in Colonel's mane, looked thru between his ears and says, "Come on, Son. Let's head 'em off."

As the track was cleared, Mansfield scrambled up the judge's stand, Cal right on his heels, and by the time they got up there and looked around the first lap was near over and Colonel had headed off many lengths separating him from the Mansfield horses. In fact there was only one length to their tail, and there was still another lap to go.

Colonel was only getting warmed up at the start of the second lap. The Mansfield horses was neck and neck and hugging the rail, well in the lead of the others and with reserve speed to go on.

Then as the shadow of the dark horse, Colonel, crowded up on 'em that speed soon begin to be used up. They soon went to their level best but it didn't seem to be of no use. That shadow kept a crowding up on 'em until it reached their flanks, then the Mansfield jockeys begin using their whips. Blackie didn't have nor want no whip.

Steadily, from the flank and a rib at a time that shadow crept up on 'em. The two Mansfield horses was still nose to nose as the shadow crept to the shoulder point, and there was still a hundred yards to go.

Then, Blackie, now with his eyes on the two jockeys and his mouth close to Colonel's ears, just only whispered. "Lets go now, Cowboy," and at that the range trained thoroughbred spurted up as tho he hadn't as yet tried to run and near folded 'em up against the rail.

When the finishing line was reached he was two lengths

ahead of the Mansfield horses, the best of his own half brothers.

It would be impossible to describe the feelings of old Cal as he drove up along the coast road, heading back for home, also of Blackie's, riding beside him. Even Colonel looked around mighty proud thru the windshield of his trailer.

Reminiscing as he drove along, Cal felt mighty happy that, besides the big winnings for all concerned on his side, he'd evened up an old score and in such a way that it made quite a dent, not only to Mansfield's purse but to his pride, for, after the race, and as Mansfield wondered and asked Cal what that horse, Colonel, was and where he came from, Cal then was mighty pleased to show him the bill of sale Brad had given him just before leaving the ranch. Mansfield was more than surprised and frowned at it as he seen it was written on the back of a registered paper, showing he was a colt from Montezuma. He remembered then, it was the little colt he'd ordered taken away and sold on account he was off color from Montezuma's other colts and would be a blemish to them. He felt more than mortified, and that had pleased Cal some more.

As they drove along the smooth highway, Blackie begin to notice signs advertising a rodeo. He'd first noticed 'em at the back of some passing cars, the dates and location. They would reach that town about the middle of the next day and the contest wasn't to start until the day after that.

Seeing such sign after sign got to bearing on him,

and as they stopped in a little town on the way for the night, and before he unrolled his bed in the feed corral and by Colonel he had to come out with it and ask Cal if he'd noticed the signs advertising the rodeo.

"Sure," says Cal, with a suspecting grin, "want to see it?"

"I sure would like to," says Blackie, "and more than that, I want to enter and contest in it."

Cal rubbed his chin for a spell. "It's a five day contest, Blackie you know, and if you aim to reach the finals why——"

"Yes, I know," says Blackie, "I know how anxious you are to get back home, but——"

"But *you're* not." Cal added on. He put his hand on Blackie's shoulder. "Well," he says, after a spell, "you've sure earned a good stay away and I'm sure the warden wont care. As for me I'll enjoy it all with you, bet your life. Let's whoop 'er up. We both ought to celebrate some."

That was more than agreeable with Blackie, and the first thing he done on arriving in the Rodeo celebrating town the next day was to enter in the saddle bronc riding contest. He was itching for just that only, and didn't enter in any other contest.

A good big box stall for Colonel and another next to him wher Blackie throwed his bed roll and all was set for the fireworks. Cal and Blackie took in the town, and mixing with the cowboys who'd come there to contest, many of which they knew, it wasn't long before they got in right good spirits. Many of them cowboys knew and had contested on Cal's rodeo stock. He was made more than welcome, and when the committee learned he was in town, knowing he'd won the big race, they sort of kidnapped and bowled him over with honors.

In all that commotion, Cal and Blackie got separated, and when Cal went to the stables the next morning and seen no sign of him in the box stall next to Colonel his heart missed a few beats, but it was just for the time, for he wouldn't believe that Blackie would do such a thing as break his trust. Still, he thought, with such a good chance and so far away from his *barred* stall it would be quite a temptation for any man to resist.

He walked over to the rodeo grounds where many of the boys had gathered and asked a few if they'd seen him. None had.

He was about to leave the grounds, and going by the head quarters when a feller hollered at him, saying that somebody had just called up wanting to know if Goodwin was here, and if he was, "for Pete's sake, hold him."

Cal was mighty relieved and easy held. Soon enough Blackie, near out of breath, showed up.

"Didn't know where in samhill you went last night," he says. "Been looking for you ever since."

Come to comparing notes they'd been going in circles right around looking for one another. Blackie had just got thru caring for Colonel that morning and hadn't been gone but a few minutes when Cal came looking for him, and him gone to make another round looking for Cal.

Well, that was that, and as they talked on they went

to the corrals, by the chutes, to look at the rodeo stock.

Blackie rode that afternoon, in the tryouts, on a good tough horse and qualified for the semi-finals. He done as well in the semi-finals and qualified for the finals. There was a couple of day's waiting between each ride, and he now wished he'd entered in more events, such as bareback bronc riding and steer riding, just to keep in action. But it was too late now to enter in them events.

The last day of the rodeo came. He rode for the finals, and surprised the judges, other contestants and all how that little cowboy could ride, but size dont count when it comes to riding. Blackie made the finals in good shape, and now, him and only six other boys was up for the grand finals.

Blackie pulled his hat down tight, pulled his chap belt up some, and when his name was called, climbed down the bucking chute and into the saddle, on top of a grand final horse. It was the pick of the roughest, which means the same in that game as speed does in a race, winners.

The horse was a little dirty gray, and when the chute gate opened there was no hesitation from that horse. He started bucking right in the chute, which is mighty dangerous for the rider, legs and body, and in watching out for that does not get a fair sitting.

Some of the boys spooked the little gray out of the chute. He was a spinning bucker, about the hardest kind to ride, but this one was still harder, for instead of just spinning, every hard and quick jump he landed was a spin back, no forward bucking jump.

The little gray hardly left the chute and didn't cover much more than
ten feet of ground in his bucking

The limbering up at the race, even tho it was plain riding, is all that saved Blackie in that ride—a man cant be in a prison yard and cell a couple of years without getting stale some.

Another thing that saved Blackie was that he rode by the feel of his horse and not by grip nor main strength. The hardest bucking horse for him to ride was a "straight-away," where it was just the opposite with most riders.

According to the judges, and even with the boys he was contesting against, all agreed Blackie made a great ride, taped spurs away up on his shoulders, which he had to do in order to make that ride, and which also added up on points. The little gray hardly left the chute and didn't cover much more than ten feet of ground in his bucking, but what all he done in that small space made even the watchers' heads swim.

The judge's whistle blew, calling it a ride, the pick-up man rode up, but the little gray was still at it, and whirling so fast that he couldn't get to reach the bucking rein. Then everything of a sudden got hazy for Blackie and the next thing he knew he was down to good solid old Mother Earth, grabbed himself two handsful of it and et some.

Cal was right there and the first one to him, but Blackie was right up on his feet, and even tho considerable dizzy, made it to the chutes, to lean on 'em for a spell. When the timbers of the chute got to looking straight again and the world right side up, he turned to Cal who was right near him and says.

"I want to take a look at that horse."

He started acrost the arena to another corral where the ridden and would-be ridden buckers was unsaddled and turned loose into. Cal went on with him. Many buckers was in that corral as many as there'd been rides, and as that was the last day of the contest there'd been many rides.

The two, in looking at the horses, had nothing to go by excepting the color of the horse, and they got very little chance to see that. The pick-up man came in with another horse and Blackie asked him.

"Which horse did I just ride, or ride at?"

The pick-up man laughed and pointed him out. Blackie had lost his dizziness by then. He squinted at the little dirty gray, then turning to Cal, he says.

"Do you see what I see?"

Cal was doing some powerful squinting himself at the time, but hardly dared believe his eyes.

"It cant be Charro, can it?" he finally asks, puzzled.

"It sure can, and is," says Blackie, mighty positive.

The last grand final ride over, Blackie had the pick-up man rope the little gray (Charro), not so little now but little as compared to the fourteen hundred pound bucking stock that was being used. Blackie went along the rope to the gray's nose. A signal pull on the rope for slack and he had a half hitch on that pony's nose.

But the pony was mighty outlaw. Blackie then jerked the half-hitch off his nose and says to the pick-up man.

"Haze him to the chute, will you? I want to get a

close look at that iron (brand) on him and I dont want to have to throw him for that."

In the chute the iron was looked over. It was ᵔᵔ.

As Cal was close, Blackie pointed at the iron and asked him. "Can you make out yours there? Whoever changed that iron was no artist at it and felt safer in getting him out of the country."

There was of course no doubt but that the horse had been stolen (even amongst wild horses a branded horse belongs to the owner), and Cal's aim was to lay his claim on him. He was on the "prod" (fight) as he headed for the headquarters, Blackie right beside him, on the prod too.

But the prod was took out of 'em as they entered the offices and all was paying off, for, as Blackie showed his fizog alongside Cal he was greeted so that it took the pins from under him, also Cal's, and Blackie was presented with a silver and gold flowered trophy about his arm's length. At the same time, judges and all being there, he was acclaimed the champion bronc rider.

Cal was as happy as Blackie was with the winning of the more honors, but Charro and the getting of him was still on his mind, and being elated over Blackie's ride he was more than ever for getting that little gray. It would be another winning of his and Blackie's to take home, and make Virginia and all the more happy.

The stock promoter for the rodeo was at another desk, getting his money, and Cal spotting him, left Blackie with his tall trophy, prize moneys, honors and all to see that gentleman.

Cal didn't chew his words as he come to him, straight to his elbow, and says. "Mister you have a horse in your bucking string that dont belong to you."

This gentleman took that kind of easy, and while he counted his money, not even looking at Cal.

"So," he said, "what horse is it?"

"You call him Cream Puff in your string," says Cal, "but my name for him is Alexander the Great, and I've got my iron on him to prove it, I can see it right thru that reversed ꙅ and do you know, young man, that there's quite ᑦ some penalty for anyone who buys stolen stock?—the same as the one who steals 'em."

At that, the gentleman stopped counting his money and looking at Cal.

"Are you accusing me of buying stolen stock when I know they're stolen?" he asks, up on his toes.

"Well," says Cal, "I'm not in the habit of accusing anybody in any way, but it would behoove you well, especially the way you're acting, to turn that horse back to whoever owns him. That's me."

"Why," says that gentleman, "what proof have you got he's your's?"

Cal had to laugh. "You can read brands, I know, you could ᑕ see thru that brand that it was originally the ᑕ . Any stock inspector here or anywhere can see that, and besides I've got witnesses right here to prove to you that he's my horse."

It was at about that time when Blackie, breaking loose from handshakes and congratulations sidled up alongside of Cal. "And," he pipes in smiling sort of serious, "anything you say can be used against you. *I* know the horse."

There was a few more backed him up on that, and with Cal at that gentleman's elbow this gentleman forgot to keep counting his money, and bellered.

"Why, he's the best bucking horse I've got, he never was rode before until this little black monkey"—pointing at Blackie—"came along."

"Cant help that, Mister," says Cal. "We aim to get what's ours. But," he added on, "if you want to serve the same term as the ones who stole the horse, that's your privilege."

There was no more argument. In fact, that feller was glad to just keep on counting his money, before he said, "Take him away."

"And I dont need no bill of sale either," Cal answers back. "In our country we hang fellers who deals with anybody's horses but their own."

That was the parting words. That evening, while it was still light, and before the bucking stock was taken out of the grounds, Blackie drawed his loop up around Charro's neck, snubbed and slipped a hackamore on his head, then, of a sudden, as peaceful as that wild horse was outlaw, he followed Blackie out of the corral.

In a short time he was loaded in the two-horse trailer, right alongside of his old pardner, Colonel. He fought and snorted some before getting in the trailer but soon as he got alongside of Colonel, and Blackie and Cal closed the tail gate on the both, he drawed a long breath of ease.

By the time the sun came up the next morning the four, two men and two horses, had only one more day's drive to get home on. That was done in good time over summits during the cool of the following night, after all had rested and fed during the heat of the day.

It was during that third night's driving that Cal, glancing at Blackie as he drove, remarked, "That trophy of yours, Blackie——"

"Yes," says Blackie.

"Well," Cal went on, it means a lot more than just that, it's what it might hold, and to my knowing, with the ribbons and winnings, the square and good way you done it in the race and rodeo why I know that all is near as effective as if the warden himself opened the gate. Me and him'll see to that."

As the two talked on of the past weeks' events there was two ponies back of 'em, shoulder to shoulder and bracing one another while the car wheeled 'em around the mountain curves. There didn't need to be no talk with them two, they'd always be all for each other, and masters at their own different games.